TIMBA COMES
HOME

Also by Sheila Jeffries

Solomon's Tale
Solomon's Kitten

TIMBA COMES HOME

Sheila Jeffries

**SIMON &
SCHUSTER**

London · New York · Sydney · Toronto · New Delhi

A CBS COMPANY

First published in Great Britain by Simon & Schuster UK Ltd, 2015
A CBS COMPANY

3 5 7 9 10 8 6 4 2

Simon & Schuster UK Ltd
1st Floor
222 Gray's Inn Road
London WC1X 8HB

www.simonandschuster.co.uk

Simon & Schuster Australia, Sydney
Simon & Schuster India, New Delhi

A CIP catalogue record for this book
is available from the British Library

Hardback ISBN: 978-1-4711-3762-4
eBook ISBN: 978-1-4711-3764-8

Typeset in the UK by M Rules
Printed and bound by CPI Group (UK) Ltd, Croydon, CR0 4YY

To Hayley

Author's Note

In this story you will find references to ley lines, earth energies and golden roads. I believe these are an ancient network of energy lines which criss-cross the Earth, linking sacred sites such as stone circles, churches and holy wells. I have studied these mysteries for years with the help of the late Hamish Miller who taught me to dowse, and by reading the work of Alfred Watkins, Kathleen Maltwood and John Michell.

The White Lions of Timbavati are real, and I was inspired by reading *Mystery of the White Lions* by Linda Tucker and *The White Lions of Timbavati* by Chris McBride. I appreciate the information given to me by my wonderful friend, Rose Shuttleworth, who drove across Africa to see the White Lions.

The house was full of Ellen's love, and now my wonderful kittens were playing upstairs. No matter what Joe did, the house would always be good. I'd lived two lives here now, and it was home.

These thoughts amplified my purring, during the time of sunset with Ellen. Sadly she couldn't understand them, but I could understand her human speech and what she was saying came as a deep shock to me. 'We've got to sell our house, Solomon. We're leaving,' she sobbed. 'And I don't even know if we can keep you.'

I didn't want to share the dreaded cat basket with Jessica. Joe had caught her by the scruff, bundled her inside and slammed it shut. She turned round and stared out at everyone, her beautiful eyes desperate. I sat close to the basket, kissing her through the hard iron bars, trying to calm her down, but she wouldn't be pacified. She was frightened, and broken-hearted. Her three lovely kittens had gone out in that same cat basket the day before, and Joe had come back with it empty. 'You did take them to the cat sanctuary, didn't you?' Ellen asked. 'Course I flaming did. What d'you take me for?' Joe said angrily. He was in an ugly mood, slumped on the sofa with his head in his hands. 'Just leave me alone, will you? It's bad enough losing our home without you starting.'

I looked at him sceptically. What had he done with our kittens?

Extract from *Solomon's Tale*

TIMBA COMES
HOME

Chapter One

SOLOMON'S BEST KITTEN

'I hope you're not alone.' The young woman spoke to me from the window of her red car. She must have seen my tiny black face peeping out of the grass at the side of the road. We stared at each other, and an overpowering feeling stirred in my sad heart. I was an abandoned kitten, and this young woman with the mane of bright hair was the person I wanted to be with. And she needed me. Her sweet, compassionate face was haunted with stress, as if she hadn't got time to stop, even for a fluffy black kitten. 'I'm sorry, kitty. I HAVE to get to work. You go back to your mum-cat.'

How could she know my mum-cat wasn't there?

'Please stop. Please pick me up. I'm in trouble.' I sent

1

her that thought, and my hungry meow sounded like a scream.

'Angie will come back and check you out later, you little darling,' she said. 'And if you're still here, I'll take you home . . . Oh damn!' she cried as something went wrong with the car. 'Damn this car. Come ON. I'm late for work.' She forgot about me as she struggled with the problem, revving the engine and filling the lane with black smoke that made my eyes sting.

Disappointed, I shrank back into the thick grass. My legs wobbled, and I lay down, too weak from hunger to move any more. I hoped Angie would come back for me. She had to. Didn't she?

But the next minute a stone flew out of the air and landed close to me. I jumped, then trembled as running feet pounded down the lane. Breathing hard, a boy reached down and snatched the stone. He chucked it at some boys who were riding past on bikes. They were laughing at him and calling him names.

'Leave me alone,' he yelled back. 'You bullies.'

'Leroy's a loser!' they chanted.

I crouched there, too petrified to move as the bikes skidded to a halt, sending crumbs of mud flying over my fur. The biggest boy got off his bike and shoved Leroy into the prickly hedge, pushing him again and again into the brambles until he was crying bitterly. Laughing, they rode off and left him there, wiping the blood from his face with his sleeve, and tearing his clothes on the brambles. 'My mum'll kill me,' he howled, pulling a long thread from the front of his sweater. He sat there in the mud, sniffing and shaking, and kicking the ground. I offered him a tiny meow of comfort, and immediately wished I hadn't.

'WOW!' he gasped. The crying stopped, and Leroy's big eyes stared at me. His rough hand reached out and grabbed me round my skinny little tummy. He held me up close to his face and I saw the anger draining away, and a look of pure delight dawning in his eyes. 'You're MY kitten!' he announced, and pulled a stretchy red-and-white sock from his bag. I screamed and struggled, but he stuffed me inside it, right down into the toe. My fur was squeezed flat, my legs twisted as my claws caught in the fabric, my tail hurting. I prayed for Angie to rescue me, but she didn't. Trapped in the boy's football sock, I was bundled into a bag and bumped up and down as the boy ran. Then I heard a bell ringing and the sound of children.

I listened carefully, sensing that Angie was there amongst them, and suddenly I heard her bright voice. 'Will you sit down, children, please?'

'Miss! Leroy McArthur's got a kitten hidden in his football sock.'

'WHAT?'

'He has, Miss. I heard it meowing.'

Terrified, I crouched inside Leroy McArthur's red-and-white football sock, quiet now because I had no energy to meow. Three days without food and the shock of losing everything I loved had left me too stunned to move. A sustaining flame of pride burned in my heart. I was the best of Solomon's three kittens, my long black fur glossy and soft, my baby eyes still bright blue.

'Open your bag, Leroy. NOW, please, and show me this kitten.'

The young teacher's bubbly voice stirred a memory, buried deep in my consciousness, of another lifetime. I had been Angie's pampered cat, her healer, and her one true friend.

I felt her lifting the sock into the light.

'It might be a dead rat, Miss.'

She eased me out and cradled me in hands that had crystal rings and fingernails painted jet black. The air shone with the rainbow auras of children crowding around me.

'Aw!' they chorused when they saw me peeping out, and their love made a cushion of compassion for me. I managed a plaintive little squeak.

'How could you do this, Leroy? To a kitten!'

'I didn't do nothing, Miss. It were lying in the grass.'

The boy's scratchy voice made me look up at him. I stared, transfixed, into Leroy McArthur's eyes, and a darker memory loomed. Long ago, in that distant lifetime, he had hated cats.

'It's my kitten, Miss. I found it,' he said, 'and I were gonna take it home and feed it. Me mum won't mind, honest, Miss.'

I didn't want to be Leroy McArthur's cat. Beyond the glaze of his eyes lurked bitterness that would manifest as bullying, with me as the victim. I was only six weeks old, and proud of myself so far. How had my life gone so wrong?

It all began when we three kittens lay cuddled up to our mum-cat, Jessica, in a cosy basket under Ellen's bed. A beautiful lady came to visit our dad, Solomon. She was so full of light that all of us wanted a touch or a word from her. Quivering with excitement, I sat close to my brother and waited while she focused on my pretty tabby-and-white sister. 'This is a special kitten,' she said tenderly. What would she say about ME? I was the biggest and the best, my black face bright with anticipation.

But she ignored me – and my brother.

I was livid.

When she had gone I felt the sting of jealousy. I growled at my little sister and smacked her face with my paw. Jessica gave me a disapproving swipe. It wasn't fair! Angry, I made up my mind to binge on food and grow into the strongest, most independent cat on the Planet.

Being ignored is the ultimate put-down, and seeing my brother's disappointed face strengthened my resolve. He was smaller and sleeker than me, and he had a white dot on his nose which gave him a wistful look. He was hyper-sensitive and vulnerable. I felt protective towards him. In that moment of intense humiliation we bonded for life.

We rubbed cheeks and licked each other's faces. We slept curled into each other, our limbs entwined. I could feel my brother's rapid heartbeat, and he could feel mine. The thoughts we had flowed together as if we were one. What if nobody wanted a black cat? We had each other, and in those weeks of babyhood we grew ever closer. To be separated would be unthinkable. Together for ever. Two black kittens against the world.

Days later our family was cruelly torn apart. We three kittens ended up abandoned in a hedge at the side of a country lane, closely observed by a bunch of chirping sparrows, a blackbird and two hungry crows. At dusk an owl glided low over the grass. On silent wings it swept up and down, turning its predatory face to look directly at me as I peeped from our hiding place.

We survived without our mother for a few days and nights. It was me who found a nest of dry grass to keep us warm, me who encouraged my brother and sister to lap water from puddles and taste whatever we could find to eat. I was the leader, and proud of it.

Fear is powerful. It can turn moments into eternity, and strength into panic, and panic into fury.

The dog was a hefty Labrador, her coat glistening black. I hissed and spat at her, but she took no notice. I could only watch in helpless rage as she picked up my beautiful tabby-and-white sister and bounded off with her dangling from her mouth. My brother and I huddled together, trembling as the kitten's piteous cries got fainter and fainter.

Those cries haunted me, for we'd heard our mum-cat crying when we were snatched away from her. Loud and echoing, as if Jessica wanted to fill the skies with the injustice of having her mother-love cut down so ruthlessly. The man, Joe, who bundled us into the cat cage and dumped us, had once held me in his hands and gently stroked me with a big rough finger. He wasn't cruel, just desperate and drunk.

My dad, Solomon, had explained to me how humans live such complicated lives. They don't forgive each other like cats do, so their mistakes grow into huge destructive energies which roll on across the years, hurting everyone, even tiny kittens who are full of love and joy.

I kissed my brother on his nose, and licked his sleek

head to reassure him. Our sister had gone, but we had each other. I told him we'd find a way to survive, but he didn't believe me. We were still tiny. Our claws were delicate, our fur so fine that it hardly kept us warm, our tails were optimistic little triangles, our legs wobbly and soft, inadequate for the hardship we now faced.

Pressed together we listened in horror to the sound of the dog returning, her rough paws scratching the tarmac. She hadn't brought our sister back. Obviously she had killed her with one crunch of those eager teeth. Before we had a chance to escape, the dog came crashing into our hiding place.

My paws turned into steel, and my mouth into the mouth of a dragon. Spitting and screaming I launched myself at the dog's face. With my claws embedded in her soft, bristly muzzle, I kicked furiously with my back legs. The dog just shoved me aside as if I was nothing. She picked up my beloved brother by the scruff, and the last I saw of him was his wild and desperate eyes looking into mine as he was carried off down the lane.

His cries faded away, and the silence was a new kind of silence. Prickly, like a thorn bush. Entangled in its pain, I felt the loneliness curl around me. To face so much so young seemed overpowering. Grief. Abandonment. Hunger. Danger.

Small as I was, I didn't intend to let that dog take me.

The trot-trot of her paws as she came back down the lane sent me crawling deeper into the hedge, my mind working frantically to find a solution. A hole! That's what I needed. A hole so tight that her head wouldn't fit in there.

Under the hedge the ground was crisp with old leaves and twigs, clumps of tangled plants and sprays of tough grass, impossible for an inexperienced kitten to negotiate. I stumbled along, banging my nose until it stung. Instinct told me hiding involved keeping quiet, but my distress was so intense that I couldn't help meowing.

From under a fern, I listened, and the dog stopped too, listening for me, wondering where I was. I knew she would track me, and I heard the snuff-snuffle of her nose, a whine of excitement as she picked up my scent. I crawled on, in and out of knobbly roots and branches, my heart beating crazily. There was a splintering sound of twigs breaking and the dog pushed into the hedge, shaking it right to the top, sending sparrows fleeing in a burr of wings, and the blackbird shrieking his alarm call.

I felt her determination. She was going to have me.

Well, I could fight! I was the son of Solomon and Jessica, two amazing cats. Surely their legacy of wisdom and courage would help me now.

In a hollow under the hedge was a pile of rubble. Broken glass, blue plastic and jagged lumps of concrete. I clambered over it, cutting my paw on the glass. Sticking out of the rubble was a pipe. Old and dirty, but perfect! I crept inside, down, down into the dark, just in time. The dog's hot breath gusted after me. She barked, and the sound jolted the pipe and vibrated through my fur. Trembling and weak with exhaustion, I struggled to turn round in the narrow space. It hurt, but I managed it, and crouched there, glaring out at her.

She stuck her nose into the pipe, and I saw a twitch of whiskers and a gleam of red in her brown eyes. But I was safe. She couldn't reach me. Frustrated, she began to dig furiously, thumping with heavy paws. Idiot, I thought. Wasting energy tearing up the earth. From that moment I despised the entire dog population of the Planet. Wait until I'm big, I thought. No dog is ever going to frighten me again, and I visualised the magnificent fluffy tomcat I would become. Golden-eyed and glossy, and gorgeous.

Inspired, I dared to advance up the pipe and aimed a mini-slash at her nose where I knew it would hurt. A blood-curdling yowl emerged from my mouth and my fur sprang to attention, making me look twice as big and spiky.

The dog's yelps of pain were music to my baby ears. She backed off and sat there staring and huffing. The stench of her breath made me even angrier. I sent her a telepathic message. 'Leave me alone, or I'll come and beat you up when I'm big.'

She whined, and seemed to be trying to explain something to me, but I refused to listen. Traumatised and alone, I focused on an awesome thought that shone into me like a beam of light. My life was worth fighting for, and I was here in this world for a reason.

I remained in the pipe for a long time after the dog had gone. The warm afternoon sunshine and the hum of bees in the clover flowers made me drowsy. When I awoke from a snooze, my guts ached with hunger. I longed for the sweet taste of Jessica's milk, and wanted her to be there, washing me and purring.

I tried to meow, but no sound would come. I tried to go out and search for food, but my legs were weak. My strength had gone. I was hungry, lost and all alone.

My baby teeth weren't strong enough to eat ladybirds and slugs. As twilight came, I watched a moth crawl out of the grass and figured it might be something soft for me to eat. It glanced at me with contemptuous orange eyes and flew away on wings that purred like a cat.

The moon was rising, changing from a rosy pink to a sharp white gold. Now very weak, I just lay there watching the night sky. My body was pretty useless, but in my mind something was happening, a light brighter than the moon was waking me up, making me remember.

Solomon had told me cats had lived on Earth for

thousands of years. He had told me about an invisible power called love.

So I listened. I gazed at the moon and let it soak into my lonely soul. I saw a light, greater and brighter than the moon, and with energy fizzling around it. I sat up, my hunger forgotten, my loneliness unimportant now as I waited, spellbound, for something to happen.

But what came padding towards me out of the light was a complete surprise.

It was a lion.

A White Lion with a mane that rippled like water. The luminous fur seemed charged with electricity, and barbs of dazzling light pulsed around its edges. The moths and creatures of the night vanished into the stillness. No twigs crackled, no grass rustled, no owls hooted, no rain pattered. Even the wind in the corn was silent, becalmed by this phantom creature from the spirit world.

I thought I was going to die. Or was I dreaming?

When the Lion's eyes found me, I was hypnotised by their power. I managed to stand up. I walked towards him with my tail up, and lay down in the cocoon of light between his mighty paws, and he was SERIOUSLY SOFT.

We purred together, a tiny kitten who might have been dying, and a White Lion who had come from the spirit world – for ME!

I didn't know what would happen next, or what I would do when morning came. I gave the last sparks of my energy to listening. Intense listening.

The eyes of the great White Lion burned with a secret he would tell me, if only I had the patience and faith to listen. A long time passed, and at last the words came, drifting out of him like magic seeds from a dandelion clock.

Words I would remember for ever.

Chapter Two

LEROY MCARTHUR'S CAT

An abandoned kitten doesn't have rights. Humans can make terrible decisions about where and with whom it will live.

There'd been a row between the young teacher, Angie, and Leroy's mum, Janine.

'Findings are not keepings, Leroy.'

Angie was small for a human, and she reminded me of a squirrel as she stood there all bushy with anger.

'They are for the likes of us,' Janine hissed. 'We don't have money in the bank. I have to watch every penny. Leroy can't have nothing he wants . . . nothing.'

'So how can you afford to feed a cat?' demanded Angie.

'Cats don't need much,' declared Janine. 'We had cats when I was a child and they lived on scraps.'

SCRAPS! I didn't like the sound of that. It didn't fit with my plan to grow into the biggest, fattest, most independent cat.

'This is a very young kitten,' Angie said. 'He's lost his mother and his home, and he's weak. He needs feeding up with proper kitty milk . . . you get it in a tin from the pet shop, and mix it up. . . it's specially formulated for weaning kittens.'

Janine snorted. 'Well, I can't afford fancy stuff like that . . . good old cow's milk will have to do.'

'I'll be happy to get you a tin of kitty milk . . . as a gift,' Angie said. 'And I'll get you some sachets of proper kitten food. You can have it on me.'

Janine puffed herself up. 'No thanks. We don't need charity.'

'It's not charity. I'm just concerned for this little kitten's well-being.'

'And I'm not, I suppose? I don't want no bloody handouts from the likes of you. You don't know NOTHING about how we have to live.' Janine edged closer, her shoulders squared for attack, her face drained and joyless. 'I want my Leroy to have the same as his friends.'

'I ain't got no friends, Mum,' Leroy piped up.

'Be quiet.'

16

'This kitten's gonna be my friend. Aren't you?' Leroy said, and his small hands clutched me so fiercely against his heart that I squeaked in alarm and tried to escape by crawling up his sweater.

'I said shut up. NOW. And don't let him ruin your school jumper.'

'But I love him. I do, Mum.' Two gleaming tears ran down Leroy's cheeks and dripped onto my fur. 'Tell her, Miss.'

Angie sat down at the table, bringing her head level with Leroy's defiant stare.

'Then try not to squeeze him like that, Leroy. He's fragile,' she said tenderly. 'His little bones are like matchsticks. Let me hold him for a minute, please.'

Leroy clutched me tighter then, so tight I could hardly breathe.

'You can have him back,' Angie said, her eyes looking directly into his. 'I just want to give him a goodbye cuddle. He's so sweet.'

To be picked up by Angie was heaven for me. I snuggled into her cushiony chest, and listened for the heartbeat, steady and strong under the ruffled blouse she wore. Home. This was home. I couldn't believe she was letting me go like this . . . to Leroy McArthur! I gave her a meaningful stare, and began to purr for her. 'I want to be YOUR cat,' I was telling her. 'I belong with you.'

'He's purring. Listen.'

Leroy brought his head close, and a magical smile lit up his face.

'What about his name, Leroy?' Angie asked. 'Are you going to give him a name?'

Leroy's eyes roamed around the classroom and focused on a poster behind the teacher's desk. He pointed, so I looked, curious to see what name he was going to give me. And there, unexpectedly, was a picture of the face of a White Lion. The moment exploded into magic. My neck got longer and longer as I stared at the Lion's serious eyes. Was it MY Lion?

Leroy turned, beaming, and shouted out, 'Timba!' Then he reached to stroke me – this time gently – and he looked right into my eyes. 'Hello, Timba.'

'That's a brilliant name, Leroy,' said Angie.

'Timmy will do for me,' said Janine. 'We don't want nothing fancy.'

'No, Mum. TIMBA,' insisted Leroy, his eyes round and his voice husky with passion. 'It's cos of the White Lions of Timbavati. They came to save the world. Miss told us about them.'

Then Leroy added something amazing. 'And if he had a brother, Miss, I'd call him Vati.'

I thought about my brother. Vati: that's what his name would be. Timba and Vati. Two black kittens against the world. I remembered Vati's poetic little face, his sensitivity and the way he had always stayed so adoringly close to me. Right then I wanted him so much.

'That's a very clever idea, Leroy,' Angie said. 'I like that.'

I was falling asleep in Angie's comforting hands. Please keep me, I dreamed. I don't want to be Leroy McArthur's cat and live on scraps and get squeezed and mauled around.

Those few moments with Angie were precious. I was only a kitten, but I stared into her eyes with the mind of an adult cat who had lived many lives with her. I was searching for reasons why she needed me now. What was causing the stress? Why did I feel this beautiful, loving young woman was hiding so much sadness? I saw the burden of too much caring weighing her down, stealing her happiness. Angie was trying too hard to love. She wasn't looking after herself. She definitely needed a cat. Me!

Perhaps if I'd stayed awake, there might have been a way of escaping, but I was so tired, and the last thing I heard was Angie's voice saying, 'Baby kittens need to sleep a lot, Leroy. You mustn't try to wake him up.

'Now you must promise me you will look after Timba and be kind to him. He needs small regular meals, and a litter tray, and a quiet home where he feels safe ... Are you listening, Leroy?'

'Yes, Miss.'

'And he's got to go to the vet and have his injections against cat flu. I'll give you the name of this website about caring for kittens. It's—'

'We don't have a computer,' said Janine.

'Right. OK.' Angie looked thoughtful. She carried me over to the book corner. 'There should be a book here about cat care.'

'That's no good. He can't read,' said Janine, and Leroy hung his head and looked ashamed.

'But you can,' said Angie, pulling out a slim book with a cat on the front. 'And Leroy can read now, with a bit of help.'

'I don't have time for that,' Janine said and she pushed the book back across the table. 'I'm not stupid, you know. I know how to look after a cat. It's not rocket science, is it?'

In my dream Vati was calling and calling for me. He told me an incredible story. The dog, Harriet, hadn't hurt him or my tabby-and-white sister but carried them into a cottage where a kind old lady had looked after them and given them kitty milk on a saucer. Then he and my sister had gone to sleep WITH THE DOG! Today they'd both been delivered to a cat sanctuary, and a lady with a painted face had chosen my sister and taken her away. Vati was all alone, like me, and in the dream we established a telepathic link to keep us in touch. We'd always been close and needed each other, but now we were separated our need had become an intense ache in both our souls.

When I finally woke up it was late afternoon, and I was in a cardboard box with Leroy's woolly hat and a battered teddy bear who looked and smelled musty. I wailed in fright, and Leroy's bright face peeped in at me. 'Hello, Timba.' I meowed back, and he airlifted me out of the box and put me down in front of two dishes. One had milk, and the other had something white with orangey crumbs. The milk tasted weird and sour but I lapped and lapped until my tummy felt warm and heavy. Then I tried the other stuff. 'A bit of my fish finger,' Leroy said. 'I mashed it up for you. Do you like it, Timba?'

Leroy sat on the floor with me and talked non-stop while I sidled round the dish, trying to work out a way of eating this tough, unfamiliar food. It tasted OK, but the crumbs were gritty and the fish too chewy for my immature teeth. I dragged most of it off the dish and made what Janine called 'a dreadful mess'.

'You can't force him to eat, Leroy,' she said, but he kept picking up flakes of fish and trying to put them in my mouth.

Next, Leroy wanted me to play, and he waved all sorts of bits and pieces right in front of my face when I was

TRYING to wash. Jessica had always washed me first. I was her favourite, and her bristly tongue dealt efficiently with my long fur. Doing it myself was hard. I needed space and quiet so I crept under a table, but Leroy followed me, crawling as if he was a cat. The floor felt sticky and wisps of fluff clung to the chair legs, and there was nothing to look at. I longed to be sitting in a sunny window, or in a garden where things were happening. This was a gaunt and gloomy place.

'Leave the poor kitten alone!' Janine shrieked. 'And get up off the floor. Who's going to do your washing?'

Leroy took no notice of her. He seemed obsessed with watching what I was doing. Janine reached under the table, her eyes furious. She got hold of his arm and dragged him out, banging his head on the table edge. His roar of pain and rage frightened me, and I ran for the nearest crack, a space behind a cupboard, and squeezed in there. My washing effort was now impossible.

I peeped out, horrified at the sight of two humans fighting. Leroy was howling, his mouth open wide, his eyes and nose running, and he was kicking viciously at Janine's shins, and clutching his head.

'I hate you. You made me bang my head. You done it on purpose. You're a horrible mother and I HATE YOU.'

'Don't you kick me! GET to your room. NOW!'

'I hurt my head.'

'I don't care. You've been winding me up all day. Get out of my sight. Go on. Go!' Janine pushed Leroy through a door and slammed it shut. She leaned against it, breathing hard, while Leroy kicked and thundered on the other side. 'Bloody kid,' she muttered, her lips white with fury. She slumped into a chair and sat with her hands over her ears.

Leroy pushed his way back through the door, picked up a chair and lifted it high above his head.

'Don't you DARE,' warned Janine, but Leroy flung the chair violently across the room, knocking Janine's coffee cup off the table, cracking it into jagged pieces. The coffee poured over her magazines and splashed onto the carpet. 'Right ... that's it!' she yelled. 'Bloody well break up what's left of this place, you evil little bastard.' Jumping to her feet, she seized the broken chair and tore the leg off it with a cracking, splintering sound. Brandishing it, she flew at Leroy. 'I'll kill you!' She lunged at him, but Leroy dodged out of the way. He grinned at the sight of his mum losing her cool, and that made Janine worse. 'I'll get rid of you,' she growled. 'I'll get the socials to put you in care.'

Leroy suddenly looked devastated, and frightened. 'No, Mum, please. I'll be good. I'm sorry for winding you up ... I won't do it no more. I'll go to bed.' And he went upstairs.

'Don't give me that bullshit.' Janine collapsed into an armchair and turned on the TV. It flickered blue, then went blank. The lights went out with a snap. 'Oh no! The meter's run out. And I've no money,' Janine wailed. 'I'll have to sit here in the dark.'

She opened the curtains and the orange light from the street made a dim glow. I didn't mind the dark; in fact I found it soothing after the noise and the fighting.

What about me? I thought. I am only a kitten.

Thinking about the loneliness and longing for my brother didn't change anything. So I remembered something Solomon had told me. 'Use your tail,' he'd said. 'Humans can't resist tails. Your tail is like a smile when it's up. At the worst times, when humans really get to you, don't hide, don't sulk . . . walk out there with your tail up.'

My tail wasn't very long yet, but I decided to have a go. When Janine had quietened down, I meowed, put my tail up and walked out there.

She melted!

'Oh Timba, you're so cute,' she crooned. 'Poor little scrap . . . we weren't shouting at you, sweetheart.'

She picked me up and let me nestle into her shoulder. I rubbed my soft fur against her bare neck, and we sat together in a calming silence. The ultimate surprise was that it made me feel better too.

'It works every time,' Solomon had said.

Encouraged by my unexpected success, I listened to this angry woman's heartbeat. It sounded like tired footsteps.

A young kitten doesn't usually experience sadness, but it wasn't new to me. Already, in my short life, I'd had a bucketful. Yet it hadn't touched my spirit. I could play and cheer myself up, any time, and I was glad to be a cat and not a human. So I decided to try and comfort Janine with my love, the way I'd comforted Vati. Janine was huge of course compared to a kitten, so I focused on her neck and shoulder, giving her little licks and purrs.

'You're a poppet ...' As she stroked me she began to talk, the words tumbling out of her as if they couldn't wait to escape. 'It's no fun, being a single parent,' she confided, 'and Leroy's a nightmare ... an absolute nightmare ... always has been. I am at my wits' ends with him, and I know I shouldn't hit him, but I can't help it. I get so desperate.'

I listened, not understanding most of it, only sensing some bond I had with her, some undiscovered reason why I was there. Why me? And then it washed over me like the cold night air. I heard the word 'dump', and saw the light from the window shining through the slow-moving tears on Janine's cheeks. 'I'm so scared,' she said, 'of those social workers. They're gonna take my Leroy away ... I

25

know they are ... that is, if I don't dump him in care first.'

I got the picture. Dumping. Abandoning. How well I understood that!

'Sometimes I just want to end it all,' Janine continued. 'Take a load of pills, or pack my bag and get the hell out.'

Was that why I had been sent? To be Leroy McArthur's cat?

Leroy's tantrums happened several times a day, and usually involved a dispute with his mother. I became an expert at finding places to hide in the cluttered house. It made the time I had spent in the hedge with Vati and my sister seem happy, a time of sunshine and discovery. Here in this house, there wasn't a world. I had no contact with living creatures, no chance to observe their ways and learn. I was a kitten in prison.

Leroy couldn't leave me alone. He'd pick me up and put me in some bizarre place so that he could watch the effect it had on me. Once it was high up on a top shelf where I felt unsafe so wanted to get down. He stood there laughing while my meows got more and more frantic. Another time he picked me up when I was asleep and put me into a deep stone urn. I woke up cold, and looked at the circle of light above me. Not yet strong enough to jump out, I panicked, screaming, and scrabbling on the slippery surface.

Instead of rescuing me, Leroy looked into the urn and

shouted, 'Boo.' Then he tapped the urn with a spoon and the sharp ringing noise really upset me and hurt my sensitive ears. When Janine heard me wailing, it led to yet another row between them.

'Either you stop tormenting Timba, or he goes back. Angie said she'd give him a home if things didn't work out.'

'I'm not tormenting Timba,' Leroy argued. 'I'm just entertaining him.'

'No, you're teasing him. Can't you see the difference?'

Leroy shrugged. He picked me up before Janine did, and held me against his bony little chest. 'He's my kitten, aren't you, Timba?'

'Well he won't love you if you treat him like that.'

'He does love me.' Leroy clenched his hand until I squealed.

Janine shouted at him furiously. 'Stop squeezing him. He's not a toy, Leroy. You'll hurt him. Stop it, you stupid boy.'

'I ain't stupid.' Leroy glared and pouted.

I felt the pain rush through his young body, and it was a new experience for me. Whatever Leroy did to me, his pain was worse than mine, and it was attacking his heart.

I climbed up to Leroy's shoulder, and saw the pulse beating hard in his neck. I rubbed my head against it, and purred into his ear. He peeped round at me and smiled. For the first time I felt it was possible to love this desolate boy who seemed to be disliked by everyone, especially his mother.

Later that morning I escaped into the garden. It had long grass, piles of boxes and broken bikes. Out in the sunshine I felt alive again, smelling and listening, my whiskers twitching, my eyes following every movement. The sky felt like a blue umbrella, a friendly sheltering dome above me, and the breeze ruffled my fur. I tried to sense my brother and figure out where he was, but a different animal smell came to me from a tunnel. Intrigued, I ventured inside, following the curve of it, hoping it might be a way out of the garden, a chance for me to run away from Leroy and search for Angie.

But deep down in the grass tunnel was a creature bigger than me with a pink snout of a nose and two beetle-black eyes. A rat! I turned into a ball of wire bristles and hissed at him. He lunged at me in a blaze of whiskers and a gleam of white fangs. I fled in terror, hearing his enraged squeak as he chased me. He would kill me. Where could I go?

I shot out of the tunnel and made for the doorstep. Leroy was sitting there laughing at me. 'What's the matter, Timba?' I dived inside his jacket, settling under his arm, where the slow beating of his heart calmed me down, made me feel safe again. When I peeped out there was no sign of the rat, and I was glad to let Leroy carry me indoors. Humans do have their uses, I thought, despite their bizarre behaviour.

Chapter Three

SURVIVING

Leroy's bed was a chaotic heap of clothes, pillows and smelly old teddy bears. Without undressing or washing, he kicked off his shoes and got in, keeping me there on his shoulder as he dragged a duvet over himself. To my surprise, he went to sleep instantly, and then, in the stillness and the silence, I saw his angel.

She wasn't hovering in the air. She was all around Leroy like a shining blanket, her beautiful face close to his head. I meowed, hoping she would notice me, and she did. We gazed into each other's eyes and for me it was like drinking when you are thirsty. The radiance of an angel's eyes is limitless and sustaining. I was thrilled when she spoke to me.

'It was me who told you to purr, Timba,' she said, while I soaked up every life-giving word. 'You are a fabulous kitten, a messenger of love and fun.'

'So why have I ended up with Leroy? It feels wrong,' I said.

'It isn't wrong, Timba. You've done everything right and we are proud of you. Leroy is having a difficult childhood, like you, and he needs your love. You are a tiny kitten, I know, but your love is not tiny. Your love is huge and powerful. Your love is like an angel. Always remember that.'

As if I would forget! Her words were music to me.

'You will mature into a strong and magnificent cat, Timba. You and Leroy have a special bond. There will be happy times. You can have one right now, while Leroy is sleeping!'

She closed her beautiful eyes and her light lingered around the sleeping boy. I got up and stretched my small body. It felt flexible and re-energised. In the dim orange glow from the street lights outside the window, I surveyed Leroy's bedroom and felt excited. So many interesting things to play with. If only Vati was there with me.

Playing on my own made me use my imagination. I patted a silver bottle top and pretended it was a mouse. Even though I had never actually seen a mouse, my instinct told me how fast a mouse moved and how it dived into holes. There were plenty of 'holes' around. Carrier bags, shoes and piles of clothes cluttered the floor, creating pockets of darkness. I practised chasing the bottle top into one, then stalking it like a grown-up cat. I found a toggle hanging from a coat and had a go at leaping and twisting to catch it, not always landing the right way up, and frightening myself a little, especially with the noise I was generating. Loudest was a paper carrier bag. It crackled like thunder when I was jumping around inside it, and the sound excited me. My tail bushed out and everything became too vivid, as if no barriers existed between imagination and reality. Tense with excitement, I stood looking up at Leroy's football which seemed to be shivering all by itself. I patted it, and it moved. Was it alive? I pretended it was that dog's face, and launched myself at it, digging my claws in and kicking. It rolled over on top of me, scaring me so much that I ran faster than ever before and skidded into the slot under Leroy's bed.

Peering out at the football, I watched to see if it would move again, if it was really alive and planning to attack me, but it just sat there. The hiding and the watching made me feel lonely. What I needed was another kitten to share the experiences, someone to practise fighting and chasing with. A football was no good. It didn't squeal and kick me back.

I needed my brother Vati. I needed him so much that

the space around me seemed to be hurting my fur. Empty space, inanimate objects, dead-eyed teddy bears who refused to move. I crept out again, looked up at Leroy's sleeping face and wanted to be close to the warmth of another living being. In my sadness I no longer saw the angel, only the troubled boy who slept with a frown on his face.

Perhaps I would never be happy without Vati. We were meant to be together, like our names. Something was wrong with the world if two kittens couldn't grow up together as nature intended.

Overwhelmed by my lonely playtime, I managed to climb up the duvet and nestle down close to Leroy's face. His steady breathing calmed me. In his sleep he smiled and whispered, 'Timba,' and for once his hand touched me gently. We had survived our first day together, and for me it had been scary. I didn't think I could stand another one, not without Vati by my side. Before being abandoned, we'd begun to play and wrestle together, challenging each other, but never hurting. We'd learned how to be kind to each other, washing and licking and pressing close, and the three of us had slept in a comforting mound, our limbs tangled like the roots of a tree.

Now I had only this unpredictable boy to give me warmth and security. While he slept, I sat beside him on the pillow and made myself wash and wash until my long fur felt damp and clean. I listened to the sounds of the street outside, and they were different from the sounds I'd heard from the hedge. Humans are noisy. Banging drums, blowing pipes, twanging strings and yelling out songs. They call it music, but to my sensitive ears it was unfriendly, an unwelcome vibration that pulsed through the floorboards. Any fragments of silence were ripped apart by aggressive roars from motorbikes and cars. They gave me a headache.

My sense of isolation deepened. Rebellious thoughts crowded into my mind. Thoughts of escaping, making my own way in the world, spending my life on a journey which would never end until I found Vati.

In the morning, long before Leroy was awake, I climbed the curtains, getting my slender claws caught in the coarse threads of heavy fabric which had once been red. Like everything else in that house, the curtains smelled rancid. Determined to get onto the windowsill, I swung precariously and finally made it in time to catch the first rays of the sun on my fur.

The view was mostly of rooftops and chimneys, a few trees, lots of windows flashing in the sun, and a street full of doors where a lost kitten might find a home. A street of opportunities! I looked up at the window and noticed the top was open. Immediately I smelled the grass and the briny rivers of the countryside beyond. It was powerful.

Somewhere out there was my brother Vati. I looked down, and my heart leaped with excitement. Directly below the window was a sloping roof, its red tiles already soaking up the sun. A blackbird was there, pecking at small domes of moss and chucking them all over the place.

I SO wanted to be out there.

The open window was tantalisingly high, the glass too slippery for my paws. Today, I thought, today I'm going to practise jumping, eat as much as I can, and build the strength in my back legs. It won't be long before I'm strong enough to spring up and escape through that window. I'll be a rooftop cat, and live on birds, and sunbathe, and at night I'll listen for owls hunting over the distant fields. When I know the direction, I'll set off on my journey to find Vati.

I sat bolt upright to watch something VERY strange turning into the street. A car, a bright, optimistic red ... with an aura! The aura emanated from whoever was inside.

Astonished, I stared down as the car pulled in and stopped right next to our front door. The aura got out, and, hey, it was Angie! I meowed and scrabbled at the annoying glass with my paws, but she didn't look up. She reached into the car and extracted a blue plastic bag bulging with mysterious packets. Then she tiptoed across the pavement in a swirl of black skirts, a floaty scarf trailing bits of scarlet. She hung the plastic bag on the door handle, and tiptoed back to the car. I glimpsed her mischievous smile as she stepped in and closed the car door with a secret click. The car purred off down the street, its aura of aqua and lemon brighter than before.

I cried after her, and carefully observed which way she went. Angie was going to be part of my journey.

'Hello, Timba!' Leroy's face popped up next to me, his hands reaching to lift me down. I wondered what terrible idea he would have to 'entertain' me with that day.

The early sunshine looked inviting, I thought, but in the kitchen Janine was already angry. 'Sunday bloody Sunday,' she muttered, pushing mugs and bowls around on the worktop. 'And why is this so sticky?'

Leroy didn't answer but stood in the doorway with me clinging to his shoulder. 'You want your breakfast, Timba?' he asked. I meowed back. I hadn't yet learned what 'breakfast' was, but I was starving and it seemed a good idea to meow about it.

'Don't give him cornflakes,' said Janine. 'Look in this bag. It was on the doorstep. And you can guess who left it there . . . interfering woman. I never did like the school-teachers.'

Leroy's eyes shone. He put me down next to Angie's blue plastic bag on the worktop and looked inside. 'Kitty milk!' he gasped and took out a round tin. 'And . . . look,

Mum, proper cat food in sachets ... for kittens. Look, Timba. What do those other words say, Mum?'

'"Specially formulated to give your kitten the best start in life" ... and when are you gonna learn to read?'

Leroy arranged the sachets along the wall. They had glossy pictures of kittens looking satisfied, and one was like my tabby-and-white sister! I touched noses with the picture.

'He wants that one,' said Leroy and began to tear the top of the sachet.

'Don't be so impatient with everything,' grumbled Janine. 'And don't give him too much. His tummy is the size of a walnut, it says here.'

'What's a walnut?'

Janine rolled her eyes, but she didn't tell Leroy what a walnut was. 'Best mix him some kitty milk first.'

'I want to do it. Let me, Mum. LET ME,' shouted Leroy, and he pushed his mother out of the way as she tried to open the tin.

'Stop pushing and shoving.' Janine snatched the tin from Leroy's eager hands. 'Or I won't let you do it ... ever. Badly behaved BRAT.'

'But Timba is my kitten.' Leroy started his loud crying again. He tried to tug the kitty milk tin out of Janine's hands and it crashed to the floor and burst open. The precious kitty milk powder scattered across the grubby tiles.

In a frozen moment of horror, we all stared at it, and to me it smelled delicious. I wanted to jump down there and lick it up.

Then Janine exploded.

'Look what you've done! Look at it, you evil little brat!'

'I didn't mean to, Mum,' whimpered Leroy. He looked up at her, desperate for a spark of love to rescue him. But Janine's eyes were barren and tired. The sight of Leroy's crying face, and the milk on the floor, and me wobbling on the edge of the worktop seemed to ignite a bonfire of rage. It flared through her aura, and she screamed at Leroy, hitting out at his head again and again as if she couldn't stop. He fell against the cupboard, howling and pleading. 'Stop it, Mum. Stop . . . please, Mum.'

Shaken and afraid, I tumbled off the worktop and ran, low to the ground, searching for somewhere safe. I dived behind some bulging black rubbish bags stacked against the wall. Between the two of them, I found a wigwam of space, and cowered in there, hungry and bewildered.

I heard Leroy's feet stamping up the stairs and his loud nasal crying. The sound of Janine breathing and moaning, 'I can't cope. I can't do this any more. That kitten will have to go.'

Chilling words. I was too young to be sure exactly what Janine meant, but I sensed foreboding in the tone of her voice. The fear of it was stronger than the hunger in my belly. The memory of how I had stood up to the dog gave me courage and pride. Solomon's best kitten, the biggest and the best.

I crouched there watching her scraping the kitty milk powder back into the tin with a brush.

Footsteps thudded out in the street and went quiet outside the door. I was immediately on alert, my whiskers twitching and my nose trying to smell whoever it was standing silently out there, apparently listening, then knocking. Not friendly.

Janine glared at the door, as if it was the door's fault. She put the brush down, muttering curses. 'If it's that sodding social worker . . .'

She flattened herself against the wall, her eyes wide and scared, her lips pursed. The knock came again, louder, and Janine's legs began to shake.

Leroy appeared at the top of the stairs. 'Mum, someone's knocking at the door,' he whispered.

'Shh!' Janine held her finger to her lips and held the other hand up as if to stop Leroy. He rolled his eyes and went back to his bedroom. I stayed where I was, cowering behind the rubbish bags, getting hungrier by the minute.

The knock came a third time, insistently, and a man's voice called out. 'Mrs McArthur. Answer the door, please.'

Janine shut her eyes and pressed herself harder against the wall.

'Mrs McArthur. I know you're in there. Answer the door. You'll be in trouble if you don't.'

Still she didn't move.

'Mrs McArthur. It's Trevor from Getta Loan. You are now six weeks in arrears with your payment. If you don't pay we'll be taking legal action to reclaim the money you owe us.'

Janine just stood there until eventually the man said, 'I'm going now, but I'll be back tomorrow and I shall expect a payment.'

A piece of paper shot through the letterbox, and I heard the man walking away. Janine's back slid down the wall, and she sank to the floor, breathing in gasps and whispering, 'What am I going to DO? Oh God, what am I going to do?'

After a while she got up and resumed sweeping up the powdered kitty milk from the floor.

'Timba. Timba. Where are you?'

Janine was searching for me. Calmer now, she scuffed around in her slippers, looking under furniture and behind curtains. Thoroughly frightened, I stayed hidden. Instinct told me that a cat should not reveal a hiding place in case it was needed again. Wait until their back is turned, then magically appear, with your tail up as if everything is fine.

I waited until Janine was at the worktop, vigorously mixing some of the powdered kitty milk with water. It smelled wonderful, so I emerged, meowing, with my tail up, absolutely starving.

'Oh there you are.' She put a saucer of kitty milk on the floor. 'Here you are, sweetheart.'

I lapped and lapped, enjoying the creamy milk, even though there were lumps in it and flecks of dirt from the floor. Strength and comfort flooded into my small body. I cleared every last grain of it from the saucer, and sat back. I was so fat that my tummy swung from side to side when I tried to walk.

'You WERE hungry.'

Watching me feed seemed to bring out a different side of Janine, a tenderness. I wondered why she didn't treat Leroy as nicely as she was treating me.

Gingerly she picked me up and carried me over to the sofa. She slumped into the cushions and closed her eyes. I walked around on her spongy body, glad of a few moments of peace, away from Leroy. He had stopped crying and was bouncing his football harder and harder against the walls and floor upstairs. Every time it knocked something over, Janine tensed and her face, neck and shoulders went hard. Both of us were on alert. What would happen when Leroy came downstairs?

Chapter Four

THE OWL WOMAN

The next thing Leroy did that same day was the worst so far. In the small back garden, amongst the piles of discarded stuff, was a supermarket trolley upside down. Leaving me shut in the house, Leroy dragged it out of the brambles and wheeled it inside when Janine was upstairs.

'Come on, Timba. I'm taking you for a ride,' he said, looking at me with one bright eye. The other one was swollen shut from Janine's frenzied attack on him. He picked me up and lowered me carefully into the wire trolley. I didn't like it in there. My paws slipped between the wires and I couldn't stand up. It was uncomfortable.

'You want something to sit on, Timba?' he asked — nicely — and took my answering meow as a yes. He grabbed a red-and-white tea towel from the kitchen, folded it, and put it in the trolley. He sat me on it, but it was still uncomfortable. I didn't like it and tried to climb out. 'No, Timba. It's too high for you,' Leroy said, and kept me there. He looked up at the stairs, and listened. 'Mum's asleep,' he whispered. 'I'm taking you out in the sunshine.'

He opened the front door very quietly, and pushed the trolley out into the street. 'I got a key, Timba,' he said, and showed me a shiny thing on a string around his neck. He closed the door and I sat still on the red-and-white tea towel, sniffing the afternoon air and distant, familiar smells of grass and honeysuckle. There was the sky above me and the sun was warm on my fur.

For a few minutes I was OK and might even have felt happy, but Leroy started to run, the trolley bouncing crazily over the rough pavement. Shaken, I clung to the tea towel, meowing in fright. 'Stop, please stop!' Crying now, I sent him that desperate thought, but he didn't get it. At the end of the street he stopped by a portly red letterbox. He picked me up and held me against it, pushing my head into the black slot. 'That's where you post letters, Timba,' he said. I wriggled and kicked with my back legs skidding on the shiny red paint, terrified he was going to drop me into that hole. I twisted round and looked at him, and my eyes must have been black with fear.

'Don't be scared, Timba,' he said. 'I'll look after you.'

He put me back in the trolley, swung it round and raced down the road, scooting with one foot and smiling at the fun he was having. I clung on, now terribly distressed, my little body bruised from the hard wire. Up and down the road we went, wilder and wilder, with Leroy shouting and laughing.

Until suddenly there was alarm in Leroy's eyes. He stopped still, looking at a hand clutching the trolley. An old lady who looked like a furious owl stood blocking the pavement.

'What do you think you're doing, young man?' Two spots of angry red burned on the owl woman's plump cheeks. 'Where did you get that trolley?'

'It's me mum's.'

'No it isn't. That belongs to Tesco. It's got "Tesco" on it. And SURELY that isn't a kitten you've got there!'

'It's my kitten.'

'POOR little darling.' She reached in and tenderly lifted me out, ignoring Leroy's protests. I hurt so much that I made funny little meowing noises in my throat. I was already weak, and this ordeal had made me worse. My strong back legs felt tired, my ears rang painfully, and my paws were sore.

'You poor little angel!' The old hands were woody, like tree roots, yet they shone. Healing hands, I thought, amazed ... I've found a human with healing hands. I leaned against the woman's vast bosom, which was draped in layers of flowery cotton. Her eyes switched from compassion to disapproval when she looked at Leroy.

'It's my kitten,' he said again.

'Well, are you trying to kill it?' the owl woman thundered and Leroy looked shocked.

'No. I was only taking him out in the sunshine.'

'But it's hurting a young kitten to be banged about on that dreadful trolley. He must be bruised all over. He's stunned and bewildered. Why are you treating him like this?'

Leroy looked mortified. 'I didn't know,' he said, and began to cry, this time quietly. Silent tears of shame and fright.

'Does your mother know what you are doing?'

Leroy shook his head. The owl woman had some power over him. Her sharp eyes pinned him to the pavement. He reached up and touched the top of my head with one finger.

'I'm sorry, Timba,' he said in the faintest of whispers.

'I should think you are,' thundered the owl woman. 'I know where you live, Leroy McArthur, and you are going to turn that trolley round and wheel it home, nicely, in front of me, and I shall walk behind you and carry this darling kitten, and when we get to your house I shall want an explanation from that mother of yours.'

'Mum's in bed,' said Leroy.

The owl woman tutted. 'In BED? Is she ill?'

'No . . . and can I have my kitten back . . . please?'

'Certainly not. You aren't fit to keep a kitten and I shall tell your mother. Oh I won't mince my words . . . and if she's in bed at three o'clock on a lovely afternoon, I shall get her up.'

'Mum might swear at you,' Leroy warned.

'I don't care. Now . . . you turn that trolley round, and walk . . . go on. Walk slowly. This baby kitten is badly shaken.'

Lying in her healing hands on the long walk back was like floating in a golden bubble. I closed my eyes and purred. For the first time since we'd been abandoned, I actually felt safe.

'And by the way . . . Leroy . . . let me look at you,' she said, and Leroy paused and looked into her face. 'What happened to your eye, child?'

There was a long silence.

'Mum . . .' began Leroy, then he hesitated. 'I got hit by a football at school.'

Immediately his aura darkened. Why was he lying?

'I see.' The owl woman said no more but strutted behind Leroy, carrying me with such love, as if I was a baby bird that had fallen from the nest.

Leroy was trembling as he unlocked the front door.

47

'I'll take the trolley back to Tesco,' he said, 'but please . . . please let me have Timba back. He's my kitten.'

'No, you shall not have him back. You go and wake your mother and if she doesn't come down here immediately, then I'll go upstairs and see her.' The owl woman wedged herself in the open door, and we waited together while Leroy trudged up the stairs. We heard fierce whispering and eventually Janine came down.

'Mrs Lanbrow,' she muttered, looking shocked. 'What's wrong?'

'This is what's wrong. This half-dead kitten being thrashed up and down the road in a shopping trolley. It's terrified, and it's badly bruised. I wouldn't be surprised if it dies.' The owl woman had power in her voice, but she spoke with a quiet that seemed to spook Janine. 'And don't blame the boy,' she continued as Janine turned on Leroy. 'He's only a child and he doesn't understand. How come he was allowed to treat a kitten like that? I want some answers . . . and they'd better be good.' She lowered her voice an octave. 'Because I'm taking this poor kitten down that road to the vet, and he will want to know what happened. This is animal cruelty, Mrs McArthur . . . animal cruelty . . . and it's punishable by law.'

'She means the police, Mum,' Leroy whispered.

'Shut up, you. You're in enough trouble.'

'I can see that,' said the owl woman, and she put a

kindly arm around Leroy. 'That swollen eye looks very nasty.'

Janine opened her mouth to speak and shut it again, her face going white as the owl woman looked scathingly at her and said, 'And don't even think about saying it's none of my business. I make it my business to care about animals . . . and children . . . and I don't care what people think of me. Now then . . .' She looked down at me very still and quiet in her hands. 'I'm taking the kitten down the road to the vet, whether you like it or not.'

'Can I come? He's my kitten,' Leroy said.

'No you can't,' snapped Janine.

With a blend of contempt and compassion in her eyes, the owl woman left them arguing and swept out, billowing down the street with me now half asleep in her cupped hands. I was aware of Leroy's running feet catching up and his anxious expression. Was I OK?

I wasn't OK. In a haze of pain, I saw those I loved drifting towards me . . . my mum Jessica, my dad Solomon, and Vati's elfin face with its knowing eyes. Vati was there with me. He didn't want me to die. Vati and the owl woman were holding me in a glistening cradle, and the pain was leaving my body one sparkle at a time. I didn't need the vet. All I needed was the owl woman's huge coral-coloured aura, and Vati. Vati was wise. He would know what to do. I had to find him.

In my dream-like state, I saw myself being put gently on a soft rug under a warm light. I was limp and useless, and so sad. My self-esteem and my ambition to grow into a magnificent, independent cat seemed futile. I was now a pathetic scrap of fur.

'Where did you get this kitten?'

Three people were looking at me ... Rick, the vet, the owl woman and Leroy. I felt love from all of them, even from Leroy who was still crying silent tears. I heard him telling Rick where he had found me and how he had called me Timba.

Rick was some kind of a radiant being, and he spoke gently to Leroy. 'And how did you feel when you found Timba?'

'Excited,' said Leroy, 'cos I love animals and I always wanted a cat or a dog, but Mum never let me. I didn't know I was hurting Timba. I didn't ... you gotta believe me.'

'I do,' said Rick. He examined me with careful, shining fingers and listened to my heart. Then he said something wonderful. 'Timba is going to be a most beautiful cat. He deserves the best treatment we can give him, don't you agree?'

There was a husky 'Yes' from Leroy, and the owl woman said, 'Absolutely. . . and I shall pay the bill.'

Rick looked at Leroy with raised eyebrows, in silence,

until Leroy fidgeted and mumbled, 'Thank you,' to the owl woman.

'Well, I don't suppose your mum can afford it,' she said, and looked at Rick. 'Single parent,' she confided in a whisper.

'What I want to do,' said Rick, 'is keep Timba here for a few days. He can have rest, peace and a controlled diet, and lots of TLC, and we'll give him his jabs against cat flu.'

Leroy pouted. 'But I want him home.'

'I know you do . . . but you have to let him get better first . . . give him a chance, Leroy. OK?'

After Rick said I was going to be a beautiful cat, I slept blissfully, knowing the owl woman was with me in spirit, and so were Vati and Leroy. In my dream, the owl woman was making colours with her hands, colours that soaked into my bones and made them strong. She was mixing herbs and the aromas of sage, mint and catnip were infusing their therapy into my being. She was chanting a deep-toned song, and its resonance carried me on a long, long journey to a country where the land teemed with life and throbbed with heat. I tasted the hot dust, and saw the green twilight of plant life.

The owl woman took up a drum and began to beat it rhythmically with her powerful hands. In my sleep I felt the drumbeat pulsing far across the world to the distant country, and then I saw the great White Lion padding towards me.

For three days I slept curled up between the velvet paws of the Spirit Lion. His heartbeat merged with the owl woman's drumbeat, and with every thought-laden beat I grew stronger. The White Lion's paws never moved but held me steady in a globe of light. Below me was a cushion covered in mystic stardust, and above me the sky rippled with the blue-white tresses of the Lion's mane. He did not speak, and yet his silence said everything I needed to know.

At regular intervals, a hand intruded, and the humans lovingly persuaded me to wake up. They touched me with extreme gentleness, and talked softly to me. I didn't know who they were, but I managed to purr my appreciation, and my purr was gradually improving. They gave me tiny portions of thick, delicious milk and morsels of solid food, telling me what it was. 'This is tuna.' Or 'This is chicken.' It was YUMMY, and when it became clear that I could have my meal in peace and not feel threatened, I began to eat ravenously and meow for more. Soon I had the energy to wash, and enjoy grooming my fluffy coat. My bruised body healed, and began to tingle with life. My back legs felt twitchy and powerful. I even played a little between sleeps.

It was a time of healing and a time of learning something important. Humans could be good and kind, and sensitive to a cat's needs. Humans loved and wanted cats. Somewhere out there was a particular human who wanted ME. I hoped it would be Angie.

I heard the sound of Leroy's scratchy voice.

'Can I see my kitten, please? I want him back.'

'You can't come in here without an adult.'

'I had to cos me mum wouldn't come with me.'

'Then go back and tell her what I said.'

The girl at reception had dealt briskly with Leroy... or so she thought. Before she could stop him, Leroy bounded into the room where I was being kept. He saw me and came to the cage with a wide smile. 'Hello, Timba.'

I puffed out the fur around my face and sat up. I wanted to tell Leroy to go away, that I wasn't going to be treated like that again. But he was determined. With nimble fingers he started unfastening the door to my cage.

'He looks bigger,' he said, beaming in at me, both his eyes open now.

'You can't do that.' The girl shut the cage door and leaned against it, facing Leroy. 'You've got a cheek, coming in here. No one is allowed in here.'

'I don't care. Timba's my kitten and I want him back.' Leroy stood his ground, his legs wide apart, his fists ready for battle. 'You can't stop me.'

'OUT!' The girl lunged towards him and tried to push him out, but she'd reckoned without Leroy's warrior strength. He sat down on the floor.

'I ain't moving till I've got my kitten back. The vet said come on Thursday.'

'You can't take him without an adult. And there's a bill to pay. Now move, please, or I'll call for assistance.'

'No. And Mrs Lanbrow said she'd pay the bill.'

'All right then. I've got your mum's phone number. I'll ring her.'

'She won't answer. She's in bed.'

While they argued, I was planning my life. I wasn't going to be Leroy McArthur's cat. If he took me, I'd run away at the first opportunity. My back legs quivered with new strength and excitement, ready to leap out and escape. My time of recovery had passed, and the heat of courage flooded back into my body. If Leroy tried to bully me, I'd hiss at him and scratch his hands. I'd never let him catch me again.

The door opened and Rick the vet came in. To me he was like a human angel. His aura shone white and cool blue, and he emanated calm. He knew exactly where he had to go, what to do next, who needed him most, and it was the troubled boy sitting belligerently on the floor.

'Hello, Leroy! What are you doing down there?'

Leroy looked up at him.

'I want Timba back, and SHE won't let me have him.' He stabbed an angry finger at the receptionist, who rolled her eyes.

Rick didn't try to make Leroy get up, but sat on the floor with him, and looked intently into the boy's eyes. 'You're upset, Leroy, I can see that,' he said kindly. 'Are things not going too well?'

Leroy's mouth quivered.

'I don't want none of my toys, or computer games, or my football, or nothing,' he wept. 'I just want Timba.'

'You love him very much, don't you?'

Leroy nodded hard, great sobs shaking his small body. 'I wanted a pet all my life, and I found Timba . . . it's like he were put there for me. I never meant to hurt him, and I won't hurt him again. I promise.'

'Has anyone taught you how to look after a cat?'

'No. Me mum just shouts at me. She don't teach me NOTHING,' Leroy cried bitterly. 'And I get bullied at school all the time cos she don't wash my clothes and the other kids say I stink.'

'That's really tough,' Rick said quietly. 'So what is it about Timba that you like?'

'I dunno.' Leroy hesitated and turned his big eyes to look at me. 'It's like . . . cos when I hold him he's alive, and I can feel his heart beating, and I know he loves me ... don't you, Timba? And it don't matter to him if I'm a bad boy.'

'A bad boy? Are you?'

'Yeah.'

Rick allowed a silence, and it was full of messages, like the silence of the Spirit Lion.

'And are you always going to be bad, Leroy?'

'No. When I grow up I'm gonna change the world ... like the White Lions ... only no one believes me. I'm gonna go to Africa and save all the animals.' A fire burned in Leroy's aura, courage from long ago, and Rick sat there nodding thoughtfully. He unfolded his long legs and stood up, crossing the room in two hungry strides. My heart went cold as he opened my cage. Surely he wasn't going to give me back to Leroy?

'Come on, beautiful Timba,' he said, and scooped me into his luminous hands. 'I want to see you hold him, Leroy ... gently and lovingly. Can you do that?'

My plans to scratch and bite melted away when I saw Leroy's smile of delight. I heard myself purring and felt his heart race with joy as he held me close. Around his hands the light shone gold. It was transformational. The whole child shone with happiness ... just because of me. I was powerful!

The new purr I had developed in those few days was a precious key that could unlock the hardest of human

hearts, and a new skill was being born in my mind ...
bonding. So far I hadn't bonded with anyone except Vati.
I searched Leroy's eyes and saw the radiant soul beyond
the angry boy. My cute little tail went up and I moved up
over his school jumper to his face and touched noses. He
giggled as my whiskers brushed his cheek, and I knew I
had given him something beyond price.

'Stroke him this way,' said Rick. 'The way his fur
grows. It's comforting for him, and it keeps his fur smooth
and glossy.'

'I never knew that.' For the first time Leroy stroked
me the way I liked it, head to tail, firmly yet softly, quite
differently from how he had ruffled and tweaked me
before.

'That's brilliant,' said Rick, and turned as the door
opened. 'Ah, here's your mum.'

I felt Leroy tense defensively. The magic moment of
bonding disappeared under a rolling cloud of worries.
What had I done? Abandoned my plan to scratch and
bite, and bonded with the boy who had hurt and frightened me. Was I crazy?

'We'll lend you a cat cage to take him home in,' said
Rick, and he gave Leroy a book with a kitten on the
front. 'Can you read, Leroy? This is a really good book ...
it tells you how to care for a kitten. Here, put Timba in
the cage and you can take him home.'

What had I done? Well, I could still run away, I thought, at the first opportunity. Just wait till they open that door ... I'll be gone down the street, and this time NO ONE will catch me.

Chapter Five

SORRY ABOUT THIS

The evening passed without incident. Leroy watched me constantly. He even sat beside me on the floor as I ate my supper, with his own plate of food in his hand. He let me wash, and then played with me, chuckling in delight at my performance with a fuzzy ball tied on a string. I enjoyed it. We watched each other's faces and I learned to guess when he was going to move the string, and he learned that I liked it best when he moved it slowly. He gave me a white ping-pong ball which was brilliant fun. Light and fast, it sped across the floor and Leroy's laughter was encouraging. 'Timba's playing football!' he squealed.

The atmosphere was altogether lighter and more care-free. In a few hours of happiness, trust began to grow.

Maybe it would be OK. I was stronger now. My back legs felt like frustrated springs and my mind alert and mischievous. Leroy wasn't quite equal to another kitten, but he was getting there.

Janine was oddly quiet. She seemed preoccupied, and she didn't shout at Leroy once, but stared at the television.

'I'm going to bed now, Mum. Timba's tired,' he said.

'Yeah. OK. Night night.'

Surprisingly she didn't try to stop him taking me to bed, and I spent a peaceful night, glad to be close to the breathing warmth of another being. We slept together, a troubled boy and a lost kitten, under the wings of his angel.

Sitting on the windowsill in the glow of dawn, I turned to look back at Leroy's bedroom, and got a shock. There were pictures all over the walls, and at first they looked like scribbled lines and splodges, but suddenly I saw they had eyes. Fierce yellow eyes, watching me. And teeth! Long, hooky fangs and gaping jaws. Spooked, I sat bolt upright, too scared to move, hoping that a hard stare from Solomon's best kitten would make them leave me alone.

'What are you looking at, Timba?' Leroy must have sensed my fear. He got out of bed and picked me up. I was like a wooden cat in his arms, still trying to outstare those creatures on the wall. 'Don't be scared,' he said, 'those are my pictures of lions. Mum won't let me have paper, so I draw them on the wall. I get into trouble for it, but I don't care.' He carried me over to the biggest one and patted the wall to show me the lion wasn't real. 'See this one, Timba?' he said. 'See this big word coming out of its mouth? It says "ROAR", and I did a load of Rs to make it loud.'

The spooky feeling subsided, but I couldn't ignore the lions. So many of them. I kept seeing different ones, and I crept around the floor, looking up at them, checking them out. Would I have to live with these strange, unreal images?

Leroy picked up a box of pens from under the bed. 'I'll draw a picture of you, Timba!' he said. And I sat mesmerised as he made black marks on a bare patch of wall. 'This is your thick fur ... and now your whiskers.' He did my eyes very big and coloured them yellow. 'You're very small, Timba,' he said, 'but I'll look after you. I won't let the lions get you,' and he took me back to bed for a cuddle.

He was trying so hard to be my friend.

In the morning Janine was still unusually quiet. Leroy fed me and got ready for school.

'Look after Timba, Mum,' he said.

Janine hardly glanced at him. 'Whatever,' she muttered, and I sensed something ominous about her silence.

I washed thoroughly and had a little play. Then I slept

in a patch of sunshine that was pouring through the grubby window onto the sofa.

Sometime in the middle of the day, Janine picked me up and cuddled me. 'Sorry about this, Timba ... but you've got to go.'

Where had I heard THAT before? 'Sorry about this ...'

Then she put me in the cat cage and walked out into the street with me. I meowed in fright.

Now what?

Janine marched along in the sunshine, and went down the street where Leroy had pushed me in the trolley. She turned into the lane with the hedges, and passed the spot where we'd been abandoned. Was she going to dump me in the hedge again? I began to feel angry. Hadn't a kitten like me got any rights?

She walked on, looking at the ground, not seeming to notice the blue sky and the wind zigzagging through the cornfields. Past an isolated cottage where a dog was barking, and on towards a low building with a flat roof and lots of glass. A group of women with pushchairs were outside the gate, but Janine tightened her lips and wove her way around them.

'Can't you stop that meowing?' she hissed, but I wailed even louder. I was kicking up a fuss, telling the universe how these humans were messing up my life. The idea of being a wild cat rather appealed to me now. Mixed up with the anger was a longing, an ache in my heart. I wanted to be free to explore the amazing world, to know its creatures, its plants and its mysterious energies that cats can sense.

Janine took me into the building and immediately I recognised the smells of paper, polish and children. I remembered the rainbow auras and wanted to see them again. My meows had become hollow cries resounding up and down the corridors. Leroy would hear me and come running, I thought.

'Hello, Mrs McArthur. Have you come to fetch Leroy?' said the school secretary.

Janine put the cat cage on the floor so that I could now only see feet and not faces. What an insult. How would she like it? I was getting more and more upset.

'No ... and I don't want Leroy to know I'm here,' Janine whispered. 'But it's urgent. I need to see his teacher right now ... please. It won't take long.'

'Angie can't just leave her class, I'm afraid. Can you wait until home time? Then she'll see you.'

'I don't want Leroy to know I've got the kitten. Can I sit in your office ... with the door shut? He's making such a row!'

'Sounds like a big cat you've got in there.'

'It's just a kitten. Look!' Janine held the cage up and both women peered in at my meowing face. 'I don't want Leroy to hear him.'

'I should think the whole school can hear him!'

We waited, Janine getting increasingly nervous. Then a bell rang and I heard the sound of children. Somewhere among them Leroy would be grabbing his bag and setting off, expecting to find me at home.

I recognised Angie's brisk footsteps out in the corridor, and finally she was with us, looking in at me. 'You little darling,' she whispered and put her face close to the bars. 'Hasn't he grown!' She turned to Janine. 'So why have you brought Timba here?'

'You said you'd give him a home,' Janine said. 'I'm really sorry but I can't look after a kitten. Leroy is OBSESSED with him, and it's causing nothing but trouble. It's not fair on the kitten. So, please . . . will you take him . . . otherwise . . .'

'Otherwise what?'

Janine didn't answer but stared at Angie. I knew what she was thinking. She was going to dump me somewhere. My meows turned into screams.

'Oh darling! I can't bear this.' Angie opened my cage and took me out. 'You're so beautiful, Timba. It's OK. It's OK. Angie's got you now, darling angel!' She kissed the top of my head, and at last I was quiet. Exhausted from crying, I clung to the cardigan she was wearing, and tried to burrow my way inside it.

'Of course I'll have him,' she said passionately. 'And it

will be a for-ever home ... even though I hadn't planned on having a cat ... my life is in a state of flux right now ... but I won't let him down.'

'Thank God for that,' said Janine. 'I wanted to do the right thing for Timba ... he's had such a rotten time. Between you and me, I think that Leroy would end up killing him. We've had some real humdingers over it.'

'You do realise,' said Angie, 'that Leroy is going to be totally heartbroken. He's talked of nothing else but Timba. He WAS trying so hard to look after him. I'm concerned for him ... aren't you?'

Janine shrugged. 'That's life ... and he's gotta deal with it.'

'It's a shame.' Angie's eyes blazed with concern. 'Leroy is SUCH a creative child. Have you seen his art work?'

'No. I don't let him do stuff like that. He makes enough mess. You should see his bedroom. It's a tip. And he scribbles all over the walls.'

'Shouldn't he be allowed to say goodbye to Timba?' Angie asked. 'He's still here. I told him to wait in the play-ground.'

'No. Please ... I don't want him to know.'

But as she spoke Leroy's face appeared at the window, pressed to the glass. He looked at me in Angie's arms, then down at the cat cage. Seconds later I heard running feet and he burst through the door.

Sheila Jeffries

'Why have you got Timba?' he demanded. 'He's MY kitten.'

'Timba is going to live with me, Leroy,' said Angie firmly. 'Your mum thinks it's best for him.'

Leroy turned on Janine, his aura on fire.

'You got no right to do that,' he spat. 'You got no right to take my kitten when I'm not there. I HATE you. I hate you all. And when I'm big, I'll come and get Timba back.' He hurled his school bag across the room and charged out of the door. The sound of his crying rang in my head for hours.

'He's broken-hearted,' said Angie, and she kissed my head again. 'It's not over, Timba, with Leroy. We've got to do something to help him.'

My expectations of life as Angie's cat were based on my past-life experience of being a pampered cat in a luxurious palace, in a culture where cats were idolised. I thought Angie would be drifting around in silken robes with nothing to do but cuddle me and play with me. Wrong! I expected to be the only animal in Angie's life. Wrong! I assumed that in Angie's house I would never be frightened. Wrong!

The first thing she did was introduce me to Graham. Angie sailed down the hall with me tucked close to her heart. 'This is the music room,' she told me. 'And this is

Graham, the love of my life. Hello, darling.' She stood on tiptoe to kiss the man. 'Meet our new kitten, Timba. Isn't he GORGEOUS?'

I didn't turn round to look at Graham. One glimpse of his frowning eyes had been enough. I tried to burrow inside Angie's cardigan, while Graham stroked me with one finger.

'He's cute. Real chocolate box. Let me hold him.'

I wasn't ready, but Angie carefully lowered me into Graham's cupped hands. The frown disappeared as he felt my soft fur. I looked up into his eyes, and sensed a secret, something Angie didn't know about. It was dormant, like a hedgehog in winter, curled up, prickly and asleep. I knew that when it awakened Angie would be like Leroy . . . broken-hearted. Obviously she needed a strong loving cat like me.

I survived the introduction, but what followed was something completely new to me.

'Graham is a WONDERFUL singer,' Angie said. 'I hope you like music, Timba.'

'Cats do,' said Graham, and he handed me back to Angie. I stared through the window at an apple tree, and wanted to be out there on the grass catching insects and learning about the world.

'How's the new song progressing?' Angie asked. She looked up at Graham adoringly.

'Have a listen,' he said, and went to the super shiny black piano. He wagged a finger at me. 'Don't you ever scratch my piano, Timba.'

Angie slid her bust across the mirror-bright piano top, and gazed raptly at Graham. He played some notes, and I found them startling. Then he squared his huge shoulders, breathed in a bucketful of air, and began to sing like a lion roaring. So, so loud. It terrified me. The sound came from deep in his being, and its power teased the sensitive hairs inside my ears. It was louder than a cat could stand. It was like something reborn from the history of the earth, the howling of wolves, the boom of thunder, the wild cry of a vulture.

I wriggled out of Angie's grasp and leaped, spreadeagled, to the floor. My little legs couldn't yet land from such a height and I fell on my face in a jumble of panicking paws. I gathered my scattered limbs and fled into the garden. Graham went on 'singing', but Angie laughed her bubbly laugh.

Quivering, I crouched under an umbrella of rhubarb leaves and tried to calm down.

'That was so funny!' I heard Angie say, but Graham wasn't laughing and he had stopped 'singing'.

'Better get him in before he digs up my seed bed,' he said, and I could tell from his voice that the frown was back.

'Oh let him go. He's a free spirit now,' Angie said. 'He'll find his way around, and come back when he's ready.'

A free spirit. A FREE spirit! My mood lifted. Was I free for the first time in my young life? Free to explore the green garden and the mysterious world beyond? I needed to get a sense of direction and make a map of what would become my territory, find out who lived there, who passed through, and who might be asleep under the ground or in the branches.

Excited, I sat under the rhubarb leaves, my nose twitching, my eyes noticing every tiny movement, even the flick of an insect's antenna. I watched a ladybird working its way up a stalk, and I stared back at a hard-faced grasshopper who was regarding me with yellow eyes. The silvery purple seed heads of grasses arched out into the light where they danced and sparkled. I considered playing with them, but play was not on my agenda right now. This was serious stuff . . . adult-cat stuff.

A hole led under the garden fence, with a well-worn track, obviously used by creatures of the night I had yet to encounter. I sniffed at wisps of fur and droppings, not all of which I could recognise.

I waited, wanting to go through and see the world, but something was happening. The ground under my paws was shaking, and there was a rhythm to it, a one, two, three, four. Mesmerised, I stared through the hole and saw four huge hard round feet plod past on the other side, darkening the light that shone through. Then something snorted and a set of yellowy teeth tore at a tuft of grass, ripping it out from under the fence.

My fur bushed out with fright. My tail went stiff. I felt as big as two cats. Obviously this grass-grabbing giant had no idea that a black kitten sat just a whisker away from its nose.

I ventured through on tiptoe, my stiffened fur making it awkward for me to find room to move. Should I, who had slept between the paws of a lion, be so scared of this unknown creature? I made my neck longer and peeped out at the green field stretching away to wooded hills. The grass bobbed with yellow flowers, and to my right was a gleaming chestnut rump with a long tail swishing.

The horse must have sensed me, for it turned, snorting, its head low to the ground. I was the bravest kitten ever. Poised for a quick exit, I sat there and made eye contact. The liquid-brown benevolent eyes looked back, politely interested in me. The energy was female.

Start as you mean to go on, Timba, I thought, and I sent her a telepathic message. 'I'm the new cat in this household. I'm Angie's cat.' I felt proud of that status. Angie's cat!

The horse was not impressed. She blew a blast of hot

air at me, ruffling my fur, and sent me a message back. 'I'm Angie's favourite horse. Try not to get under my feet.'

She started to walk away, her nose skimming the grasses, then stopped and looked at me.

'You do realise that Angie is an earth-angel,' she said. 'And earth-angels always take on more than they can manage.'

I watched her meander across the field towards a group of smaller horses. I was a lucky cat. An earth-angel, and a Spirit Lion, and now a polite horse. I must be someone really special.

It felt good to rest in the barley grass at the edge of the field in the mellow sun of late afternoon. I needed to keep absolutely still, like an Egyptian statue of a cat, for I sensed a miracle was about to happen, which would link me with Vati. Stillness. Waiting.

It came silently. The air above the grass shimmered with millions of the tiniest imaginable spiders, each on a thin thread of gossamer, each beginning a magical journey. The grass was bedecked with a network of silver, and the sun made a pathway of gold stretching far away across the fields.

I wasn't sure what it meant, but Vati would know. Vati was like the other half of my consciousness. Somewhere out there he too might be watching the sun glisten on gossamer. Vati would know where the secret roads were, and how to find them when the sun went down. He would know how to feel the energy beneath his paws, and use it to bring us home ... to each other.

Chapter Six

ANGIE'S CAT

'It's only for one night. I promise,' Angie said, stroking me protectively as I lay beside her on the sumptuous pillow. I snuggled into the crook of her neck, my little paws buried in her sweet mane of hair.

'You know I don't like cats in bed,' objected Graham who was sitting up reading a leathery black book. Its fat wad of gold-rimmed pages fluttered tantalisingly when he turned them, and he noticed me watching. I bobbed back nervously, hoping he wasn't going to 'sing'.

'But Timba's just a poor lost baby. Mmwha!' Angie gave me one of her kisses.

Graham glowered and pushed his glasses back up his nose. 'Don't let him get his claws into the satin duvet.'

'I won't. He shall be a model kitten!' said Angie, and I got another kiss.

Feeling pampered and important, and with a full tummy, I drifted off to sleep.

As the morning sun rose over the woods, I sat in the window and thought hard about Vati. 'Talk to me,' I pleaded. 'Where are you, Vati?' I visualised his wistful face with the white dot on the nose.

A golden thread glinted in the sun. In the night a spider had swung out from the edge of the roof, spinning her silk ever longer, wilder and wilder, until she touched a leaf on the apple tree and clung there, leaving her lifeline stretched through the dawn as if to remind me how to find Vati.

I sent him a golden thread of love, and waited. His eyes looked into mine from across those fields where the badgers were. East, into the rising sun . . . and he wasn't far away. But in front of his wistful face were squares of wire. Vati was in a cage. He wasn't free like me. I felt his longing. I'll find you, I vowed. We shall be together again.

So profound was my stillness and concentration that I did not notice Angie close to me, sharing the sunrise. She must have understood I was in a trance that was not to be broken . . . except by food of course!

We headed for the kitchen, and I realised that Angie

was dressed in an old shirt, jeans and long brown boots. While she mixed my kitty milk she talked to me.

'I'm an early bird ... like you, Timba! I have to get up and help Laura with the horses, and the rabbits and chickens. Then I grab toast and coffee, shower, and go to work. You'll have to stay here with Graham while I'm at work ... then you'll be on your own for the afternoon when he goes to the theatre.'

I lapped the milk while she sailed to and fro across the kitchen, watering plants and putting silver spoons and shiny plates on a table. Then she flung the door open and stepped into the dew-spangled garden. She stood in the sun and lifted her arms and face to the sky.

With the door wide open, I thought some of the night creatures might want to come crowding in and share my kitty milk. So I finished it quickly and dragged my fat tummy to the doorstep. It proved to be a brilliant place to sit washing myself and observing. A doorstep was a 'between place', offering choices and helping me to establish territory.

I was learning how to smile. When Angie turned to look at me and said, 'Timba!' in a loving voice, I noticed how her long Egyptian eyes sparkled just because of me! So I put my tail up and tried to smile by tilting my head from side to side to make my eyes twinkle in the sun.

'You are the BEST little cat in the Universe,' she said,

and picked me up tenderly. 'The Universe has brought us together, don't you think so, Timba?'

At the end of the garden path was a gate leading into the drive where Angie's car was parked next to a gleaming black limo. On Sunday afternoon, Angie carried me down there to see it, helping me to understand the layout of our home.

'Try not to scratch Graham's precious Volvo,' whispered Angie. 'He likes everything pristine!'

She showed me the quiet lane beyond the drive, and pointed. 'That way goes to the main road ... don't you go down there, Timba, but you can go the other way. It leads to the woods.'

I took it all in, aware that Angie didn't know how much I understood. I wanted to tell her about Vati, but she was human, and humans have mostly forgotten how to use telepathy.

But suddenly Angie was tense and annoyed. 'Who on earth is that? Oh no ... I can't believe that woman knows where I live.'

A car turned into the drive with a squeal of tyres and a smell of hot rubber. Janine got out, dressed in black tights and a shiny black jacket. I thought she looked like a beetle.

'Don't panic, Timba,' Angie whispered, her hand

protectively on my fur. 'You go on purring. She's not having you back.'

Angie kept the lid on her anger and spoke to Janine kindly. 'Hello! I wasn't expecting to see you, Janine.'

'Yeah, I know ... sorry ... but I really need to talk to you.' Janine looked at Angie with a blend of defiance and desperation in her eyes. 'And I had the chance of a lift. This is Dave ...' She waved an arm at the man in the car. He nodded without smiling. Then he turned the stereo up and sat with his elbow out of the window.

'Ten minutes, babe.' Dave tapped the chunky metal watch on his wrist. 'I'll wait in the car.'

Angie led Janine to a seat by the garden pond.

'Timba's adorable,' she said.

'Yeah ... I haven't come to get him back,' Janine said. 'It's about Leroy. I need to ... like ... explain something.'

'I'm listening,' Angie said, and her eyes were full of love.

Janine seemed to be struggling. I went to and fro, from one lap to the other, trying to decide which of these two women needed me most. I settled on Janine's heart, and she started to cry.

'Take a deep breath, and just tell me,' said Angie kindly.

'It's Leroy,' Janine sobbed. 'I'm on the brink of putting him in care. I can't cope with him no more. I do love him. I do. But now he's getting bigger, it's one long battle from morning to night. I'm exhausted ... and not very well . . . and . . . and I'm actually terrified of my own son.'

'That's so sad for you . . . and for him,' Angie said.

'I'm under the doctor,' Janine wept. 'I get migraines and depression, and I never sleep cos Leroy gets up in the night and draws all over the walls, or he turns the TV on and watches stuff he shouldn't be watching. He's out of control. I don't know what he's going to do next . . . and then there's the bullying, it never stops, and it's always because his clothes aren't pristine and he hasn't got decent trainers. I can't afford stuff, Angie, I'm in debt . . . I had no one to turn to . . . not till Dave came along. I'm going to . . . like . . . lose my house if I can't pay rent any more, and Dave wants me to move in with him. But he won't have Leroy. I've got such a difficult choice to make.'

'That's tough, really tough. I sympathise,' Angie said, and her eyes looked sad.

'But I've partly come here to warn you,' Janine said, talking more calmly now. 'Leroy went ballistic over losing Timba. He's trashed his bedroom. He knows where you live, Angie, and he says he'll walk over here and get Timba back . . . he would too.'

A cold anxious feeling filled me as I understood what Janine was saying. Leroy intended to snatch me away from my beloved Angie.

'There has to be a better way of dealing with it.' Angie looked thoughtful.

'Not for people like me there isn't.'

The conversation ended abruptly when Graham came stalking mystically out of the house with angry eyebrows and his hair boiling up like a thundercloud. 'Would you mind turning that objectionable racket down?' he said to the surprised Dave. 'I am a professional opera singer, and I don't want my practice ruined by you and your stereo.'

The music stopped and Dave grinned out of the car window. 'Keep yer cool, mate. It's good music,' he said, and called out to Janine, 'Come on, babe. Before I get evicted.'

Janine scurried back to the car. 'Don't forget ... what I warned you ... about Leroy,' she said to Angie. 'You keep an eye on Timba. Heaven help him if Leroy gets hold of him.'

Chilling words. I felt threatened yet again. Why couldn't they just let me grow up and be a cat in peace?

When Monday morning came, Angie reminded me that she had to go to work. I was to be left alone with Graham for most of the day.

'Tomorrow I'll take you to see the horses,' she said. 'Today you must stay around the house and garden. Get used to the place ... it's your home now.'

She put me down on the doorstep and ran, her hair flying, round to the back of the house. I heard the horses making a weird noise in welcome, and a thundering of hooves, lots of squealing and stamping around. Angie was talking to them and laughing. She seemed like a flame, bringing light and warmth to every living being.

I stayed on the sunny doorstep until she returned, red-faced and happy, and before long she had changed into her swirling skirt and posh shoes. She picked me up, kissed me and popped me into a round basket with a sumptuous red cushion in it.

'You sleep, little cat. I'll be back later . . . and I shall tell Leroy how well you're doing. Mmwah!'

I hadn't planned to sleep, and the mention of Leroy bothered me. Supposing he came to get me like he'd threatened! The compelling thought drove me into the garden again to check out some hiding places. If Leroy did come, I'd be ready.

The fear got hold of me. Without Angie there the place was new and full of dangers. Graham might decide to 'sing'. The horses might stampede into the garden. Leroy might turn up. Then there were two buzzards wheeling overhead, crying their wild cry. What if the buzzards got me!

I slunk across the lawn and under the summerhouse, a dusty, brick-strewn hollow, dimly lit by a rim of sunlight filtering through the foliage. A good hiding place. Or was it? I spied a gigantic hole in the earth. I sniffed it, and, predictably, my fur started to ruff out with alarm. Hiding there would be bad news. Some kind of creature was asleep deep inside that dark hole. I retreated with the utmost stealth, and belted back across the lawn to the doorstep. Phew!

I didn't want to be a kitten any more. I wanted to be a cat. Eat, I thought, and returned to my dish where Angie had left me some tuna. I stuffed and stuffed, and staggered back to the doorstep just in time to see a scaly pair of legs descending from the sky and two vast blue-grey wings. Shockingly huge. Surely birds couldn't be that big?

My instinct took over and locked me motionless except for my fur bushing out ... again. There was safety in still-ness. Even a twitch of my ear or a blink of my eye would tell that dragon of a bird that I was alive and edible. How I wished I'd stayed on the lovely red cushion. I wanted Angie. I wanted Vati. I even wanted Leroy!

The enormous bird didn't look at me but unfurled its snake-like neck and stood on one leg at the edge of the pond, its eyes scrutinising the water while I imagined exactly what that long yellow beak could do to a kitten.

At the same time, inside the house, Graham started to 'sing'. 'Ah, ah, ah, ah, ah, ah, ah, AH.'

It was all too much for me.

This time instinct fired me towards the apple tree. In a terrible panic I fell over myself getting to it. My claws were brilliant. They hooked into the rough bark of the tree trunk. Thrilled to find myself climbing, I pushed with my back legs, on, up the tree into a flat place between two branches. I paused there, my high-speed heartbeat way out of control, my tail spiky, my eyes staring at the lofty blue-grey bird. He moved. His wings spread wide and he took off, effortlessly, and flew away towards the woods.

Bursting with pride at my achievement, I decided to make the most of it and stay in the apple tree. To find myself so good at climbing was awesome. I looked up into the tree's mossy tangle of branches against the sky. Why not go higher? I thought. The big bird had gone, the garden was quiet, and the sound of Graham's 'singing' was inside the house and muffled.

Higher up, the branches were thinner and there were multiple choices for me. Which way to go? Inexperienced, I didn't choose carefully, and, in my rush to get to the sky, I soon found the climbing difficult. The spurs of leaves and clusters of green apples got in my way, and now I was clambering precariously along narrow twigs. My balance wasn't mature enough to cope.

Climbing up to the sky didn't seem such a good idea. The blue had gone, and heavy clouds steamed over the sun. A warning breeze chilled my fur and made the branch sway alarmingly. I looked down at the lawn, and it was too far to fall. Then I discovered that turning round was impossible.

It didn't help to have a feisty little wren hopping expertly around in the tree. It kept its stubby tail up and its beak open, squawking out dreadful curses and threats. The question of how to get down became paramount. Even if I did manage a three-point turn, I'd still have to get down the steep trunk.

Jessica would have shown me how, or Vati and I might have figured it out together. Loneliness came over me like one of those clouds overhead. Extra-large raindrops began to fall, harder and faster, splashing into my fur. Soon I could feel water chilling my skin.

I was in serious trouble.

The meows of a lonely kitten are LOUD, and mine filled the garden and the land beyond, but nobody came. I must have stayed there for hours, soaking wet and scared. Occasionally someone walked along the lane and paused at the gate to listen. The thick foliage made me invisible.

The rain stopped but the leaves dripped on me and the tree shook in the wind. Graham appeared, and he wasn't 'singing'. He was calling me! 'Timba, Timba.' He brought my dish outside, tapping it with a spoon, and it had food in it . . . something deliciously meaty. I wailed and wailed.

'Where are you?' Graham put the dish down and picked his way across the wet grass. 'Surely you're not up there?' He peered into the apple tree and we made eye contact. A blessed moment, but he spoilt it by saying, 'You silly kitten.'

He walked away and came back with a clanking ladder. 'Don't you worry, little one. Good old Graham will rescue you.' He climbed the ladder and stretched out his hand to me. 'Come on, baby.' I managed to move the short distance to his hand and this time it felt warm and comforting. Humans can be awesome.

'You're soaking wet. Come on, come to Graham.' He held me firmly, put me on his massive shoulder, and climbed down to the ground. He took a folded white hanky out of his pocket and dried me with it. We stared into each other's eyes. 'I promise not to sing,' he said, and I stretched up to touch noses with him to show my appreciation.

'When I'm a cat,' I said, sending him the thought, 'I'll be your best buddy.'

'Aw, what a sweet kitten. He's so fluffy.'

'Here, you hold him.' Angie carefully handed me to Laura and I liked her straight away. She smelled strongly of horses, and her brown eyes were happy and kind. I crawled inside her jacket and listened to her heart while Angie told me who she was. 'Laura is our neighbour,' she explained, 'and she's got all these lovely horses and ponies.

Some of them are rescue ponies, and they live in the field at the bottom of the garden.'

'I hope the children will get a look at Timba,' Laura said, and I came out from inside her jacket and touched noses.

'Oh they will ... definitely,' said Angie, 'and I've invited Leroy to come to our Saturday club, if that's OK with you, Laura? He really needs a bit of horse therapy.'

I meowed at the mention of Leroy's name. I was anxious and Angie picked that up immediately. 'He treated Timba VERY badly, but only from ignorance, not intention ... I hope Timba's forgiven him ... have you, Timba?'

I did a yes-meow, which was a skill I'd been developing. I could now do yes-meows, purr-meows, call-meows, and fragmented squeaks which I used in conversation only with humans. Then there was the extended-meow, a really useful kind of wail to use in emergencies, and beyond that was the amplified extended-meow, strictly for special occasions.

'You'll be nice to Leroy, won't you, Timba?' Angie asked and I replied with a silent stare. I needed to think about that. What to do if Leroy tried to kidnap me.

By the end of the week I was much more confident. I'd met the horses, and the rabbits who were in wire runs and cages, and the chickens. None of them took much notice of me, but Angie and Graham gave me lots of attention. Graham persuaded me to get used to his 'singing' by humming tunes to me when I was stretched out on his chest. He did it so gently and I quite liked the vibration ... maybe it was his way of purring, I reasoned.

One night I became aware that all was not well between him and Angie.

She made him a special meal and put flowers and candles on the table, then rushed upstairs and came down in a slinky dress that sparkled like the night sky. I thought she looked beautiful.

But Graham didn't arrive. Angie paced between the kitchen and the front window, watching for his car. She got more and more agitated, pulling trays of food in and out of the oven, turning it on, then off.

'WHY is his mobile switched off? What is he doing?' she raged, and hurled the oven gloves across the kitchen. 'This meal is RUINED!'

I sat quietly in my basket on the red cushion, tired from my evening playtime, but I couldn't go to sleep while Angie was stressing.

It was dark outside and the candles on her table had gone out when Graham's car finally swung into the drive.

Angie was waiting for him at the door, a burning spot of colour on each cheek. Her bust and her chin were lifted high with fury. 'Where have you BEEN?' she demanded.

Graham looked evasive. 'Sorry, love, I am a bit late.'

'A bit late? It's ten o'clock, and our meal is ruined. It was ready three hours ago. And why was your mobile turned off?'

'Calm down, and let me get inside.' Graham held up his hand in a sort of peace gesture.

'Don't you tell me to calm down!' Angie had sparks flying from her aura. She flung her hands in the air. 'Not only is it our anniversary, but you knew I was cooking a special meal. I've been to endless trouble over it, Graham. It's an insult to me, it's discourteous and ... and ... ' She gave a growl of rage. 'It's an insult to the UNIVERSE to waste food and my time.'

He sighed. 'Don't go on about the Universe, Angie. I'm really tired.'

'You're tired! What do you think I am? I'm absolutely beside myself with FURY, Graham. How dare you treat me like this?'

He stalked past her and flung his coat over a chair. 'I'm beginning to wish I hadn't come home at all.'

Angie gave a howl of frustration, her fists clenched in the air. 'I give up,' she said in a high-pitched voice. 'Your dried-up meal is in the oven. Get it yourself. I'm going to bed. GOODNIGHT.'

'If you'd just stop being so angry—' began Graham, but Angie was already halfway up the stairs.

I heard the bedroom door slam and Angie cried, 'Why is the Universe doing this to me?'

It went quiet, and Graham came over to my basket. 'Hello, Timba,' he said in a conspiratorial whisper. 'I'm afraid I've been a bad boy.'

Chapter Seven

VATI

'What is the matter, Timba?' Angie scooped me out from behind the fridge and tried to stroke my hedgehog fur. 'Such big black eyes. Why are you so scared?'

Clinging to her shoulder, I stared out of the window. Sniffing around the garden was a dog, and it wasn't any old dog. It was Harriet, the dog who had taken my brother and sister.

When I first saw her I don't think my paws actually touched the ground. I nosedived into the house and fell over the mat. My chin stung from the impact. The sensation of my fur standing up by itself along my back and tail was like being prickled all over . . . losing control. Not pleasant.

Angie followed my gaze.

'Oops!' she said. 'A dog in the garden. Someone left the gate open ... probably me. You stay there, Timba. It's only old Harriet.'

She put me on the windowsill where I sat in draconian pose. What was Angie going to do? I practised growling in case she brought Harriet into the house. I watched stiffly as she went out there.

'Hello, DARLING,' she said ... to the dog! She had called that dog 'darling'!

Harriet had the grace to look ashamed; obviously she knew she shouldn't have been there.

'Where's your mum?' Angie made a fuss of Harriet and took hold of her collar. At the same time an old woman in a funny hat appeared at the gate.

'Oh there you are. Bad dog! I'm so sorry, Angie,' she said.

'No problem, Freda,' Angie said kindly. 'It's my fault for leaving the gate open. Not your fault, is it, Harriet? Lovely girl. Oh I wish we had a dog. Graham hates them.'

'But I see you've got a kitten ... there in the window,' said Freda. 'A little beauty! Where did he come from?'

'It's a long story,' said Angie.

The two women stood in the garden with Harriet firmly clipped to a lead (Phew!). The danger had passed, and it was time for me to wash and smooth my annoying fur. I couldn't hear much of the conversation but sparks were popping from both the women's auras. They were gazing earnestly at each other, and waving their hands around.

'Where did you say Leroy found the kitten?'

'Lying in the grass in Frog Lane . . . on a Friday.'

'Then . . . it has to be the third kitten,' said Freda. 'Harriet went back a third time, and she was gone for ages, but came back with nothing.'

'So what happened to the other two?'

The woman walked over to the gate and leaned on it, talking intently and quietly now. Suddenly Angie gave one of her screams. 'Oh God, Freda . . . this was meant to be! I'm going over there right now. Thank you, thank you, thank you!'

Once Freda and Harriet had gone, Angie skipped into the kitchen and grabbed her car keys and handbag. 'I won't be long, Timba. You stay there, and I might . . . just MIGHT . . . bring you a surprise.'

The key turned in the lock, and I watched, puzzled, as Angie's car drove out faster than normal. Angie didn't often go out after work. She'd change into jeans and a T-shirt and play with me, or carry me around. It was our special time before Graham got home.

I went to my dish. She'd forgotten to feed me! Where could Angie be going?

*

The Spirit Lion came to me at certain times, and in certain places, always when I was alone. On that summer afternoon, I braved the cat flap and headed out into the sunshine. In the back garden was a circle of stones in the long grass, and it seemed to be a place of mystery. It gave me a buzz to sit there and feel the heat of the sun reflected from the crystalline stones. A time to be still, and listen, and sense what was coming through the glistening light.

The paws of the Spirit Lion were so stealthy that they appeared silently, one each side of me like pillars of light. I felt him shuffling, shifting himself around me with the utmost care. Then I saw his cascading white mane, his soft muzzle, his benevolent eyes, and I felt totally safe, and locked into a trance.

The words came slowly from his ancient mind, and this time he called me by my name.

'Timba, Timba . . .' The resonance was like Graham's voice humming through me. 'Have confidence in the power you have been given. Don't be afraid. Remember who you are, Timba . . . the leader, the best kitten.'

I listened, fluffed out with pride.

'It's not over with Leroy,' he said. 'This child was born to help the White Lions. Do not hide from him. He needs you, Timba. Always go to him. Always welcome him with your tail up.'

'But I don't want to be Leroy's cat,' I said. 'I want to stay with Angie.'

'You won't be Leroy's cat, or Angie's cat,' breathed the Spirit Lion. 'You are your own cat.'

He said no more, but held me in the place of light between his paws. We purred together, and I noticed his purr was spaced out, so different from mine. But I felt satisfied with my purr ... it was loud for a kitten and I already knew how to use it to comfort Angie and Graham. Had I purred for Leroy? I couldn't remember. The time with him had been so full of fear and pain. Yet Leroy, more than anyone, needed the comfort of a purring cat.

I slept blissfully, and when I awoke the sun was setting, and Angie's car turned into the drive. I saw the red of it through the hedge. Whenever she arrived, the horses whinnied and the chickens clucked hopefully. Usually she went round to see them before coming into the house, but this time she came straight in. Her face was bright with joy, and ... she was carrying a cat cage!

I ran to meet her with my tail up.

'Hello, Timba darling,' she said, and smiled in a mysterious way. I followed her inside. She shut the door and put the cat cage gently on the floor.

And then a miracle happened.

The best miracle ever.

Angie opened the cat cage, and out stepped an elegant black kitten with a white dot on his nose.

My brother Vati!

Angie had found Vati, and brought him home.

'Oh not another one, Angie!' said Graham when he saw Vati sharing my dish. 'How many more waifs and strays are you going to bring home?'

Angie flared up immediately. 'As long as there's room in my heart, Graham. If the Universe sends me a gift, I wouldn't DREAM of turning it down. I'm here to love, and that includes you . . . you sexy hunk.'

She stood on tiptoe, wound her arms around Graham's neck, and kissed him until his aura filled with light and blended with hers. He slid his arms around her waist and held her close, murmuring words of love into her hair. Angie peeled off his jacket and flung it over a chair, then she loosened his tie and unbuttoned his shirt, all the time with her eyes locked into his.

They hurried upstairs, with Angie giggling and Graham thundering after her on his big feet. The bedroom door slammed shut and the house rang with Angie's laughter.

Vati and I went on eating.

It was a good time for him to arrive, I thought, with the house full of the energy of love. While we were eating, I had a good look at Vati. He was smaller than me, more streamlined in his coat of satiny black fur. His tail had grown, and it had a kink at the tip. His eyes were turning lemon-green and were full of secrets. I knew he had much to teach me, and I sensed a nervousness in him. He needed my leadership and courage, just as I needed his wisdom.

Vati was scared of being in a new house, so the first thing we did was wash each other. I enjoyed rubbing cheeks with Vati and licking his wistful face, and seeing him close his eyes so trustingly as I did so. As he washed me back his eyes inspected the room and he seemed to be listening to the twilight sounds from outside, and the particular creaks, drips and hums from the house itself. I wondered what he would do when he heard Graham 'sing'.

I wanted to take Vati out through the cat flap, but he wouldn't go. I wanted him to play with me, but he wouldn't play. I raced around on my own and he crawled onto the sofa and sat there watching me, and when I finally sat quietly with him, he seemed glad to have me there. I tuned into his mind and picked up sadness. Vati was sad. I asked him why.

'Nobody wants a black cat,' he said.

'I'm black,' I said, 'and Leroy wanted me like mad, and so did Angie.'

'But you're fluffy. No one wanted me. I was in a cage

for days and days on my own, and people kept looking in and saying they didn't want me. Until Angie came, and I don't know her. I don't feel I belong to her.'

I heard myself quoting the words of the Spirit Lion: 'You are your own cat.'

Vati looked stressed and bewildered.

'And why is she calling me Vati?' he asked. 'What kind of a name is that?'

'We are named after the White Lions of Timbavati,' I said. 'Angie's got a picture of them. Vati is a really important name.'

Vati didn't look convinced. He sat there looking tired, his black whiskers drooping. He crept into the corner of the sofa and went to sleep. I was disappointed. Something was wrong with Vati. He hadn't eaten much, he wouldn't go out, and he refused to play with me. I was bursting with energy, but I curled up beside him, and put my paw over his slim body. I purred, but Vati was silent, his sweet face peaceful. In his sleep he stretched out an elegant paw and curled it around my neck. That made me so happy that I didn't move and we slept blissfully entwined as we had always done.

'How sweet is that?' exclaimed Angie when she discovered us there. 'Will you look at these darling kittens, Graham?'

I opened one eye and saw her taking a photo of us on

her mobile. 'Poor little Vati . . . he's exhausted,' she said, and I remembered how I had slept for three days in the vet's place. I'd been physically, mentally and spiritually tired. Maybe it was the same for Vati.

In the morning he seemed OK. But after breakfast he went straight back to the corner of the sofa and sat with his paws bunched under himself. Angie had gone to work, and Graham strode past us on his way to the music room. I braced myself for Vati getting a fright when the 'singing' started. Today it was particularly loud, and it made me shudder. Vati must have heard it, but it didn't seem to bother him. He seemed to be in a dream.

He wouldn't talk to me. He wouldn't play.

Eventually he got down from the sofa and crept around the floor, his whiskers twitching as he went to and fro. It was odd behaviour, I thought. I coaxed him into the garden and he did exactly the same thing . . . creeping over the lawn, but stopping now and again to sit staring at the ground and listening.

'What ARE you doing?' I asked, going up to him and putting my face close. To my utter astonishment, Vati hissed at me and batted me crossly. He didn't want me! Unabashed, I tried again, and got another swipe.

'Leave me alone,' he snarled. 'You're breaking my con-centration. I need to do this.'

Miffed, I tried to demonstrate my progress with climbing the apple tree, made a mess of it and crashed to the ground, but Vati went on doing what he was doing.

As the shadow of the blue-grey wings hung over the lawn and the big bird again descended, I was desperate to warn Vati. A heron, Angie had called it. I fled to the doorstep thinking Vati would follow, but he didn't. The heron stood at the edge of the pond, his dagger-like beak poised in the air, his sharp eyes staring.

I couldn't believe what Vati was doing.

'Vati . . . NO!' I sent him the thought, but he ignored me and continued padding towards the heron . . . WITH HIS TAIL UP.

You've got it all wrong, Vati, I thought. I've only just found my brother, now I'm going to lose him again. And I waited for the terrible yellow beak to snatch my brother and fly off with him into the sky.

Vati was so cool. He sat down next to the heron, both of them keeping perfectly still for a long time. Just once I saw Vati look up at the heron, and he looked down at Vati. It was as if they were smiling at each other. Then stillness again, until Vati leaned forward to look into the pond. At the same time the heron stabbed down with his long beak. A shower of water glittered in the sunlight and the heron rose into the sky, a bright orange fish flickering in his beak. He flew away with it, on slow wings, water dripping from the fish.

Vati turned his sleek head and looked at me, pleased with what he had done.

In a burst of joy we trotted towards each other doing purr-meows, and at last Vati wanted to play. He arched his back and leaped sideways, and we chased each other all over the garden. Vati was incredibly agile and beautiful. He could leap and twizzle round and make a face at the same time. He shot up the apple tree and impressed me by turning neatly and doing a flawless jump down to the lawn. I was proud of him.

I'd never before had so much fun . . .

Tired from our wild game, we sat together on the sun-baked doorstep.

'What were you doing creeping around like that, Vati?' I asked.

'Don't you know?' he said, and studied me with mystic eyes. 'I was checking out what was happening under the ground.'

'What do you mean?'

Vati gave me a pitying look. 'Follow me,' he said, and took me on a tour of the lawn, according to Vati. 'Exactly here is a sleeping badger – I can feel his energy. He's deep down, and the entrance to his home is under that summerhouse . . . and he's lonely. His mate was killed on the road, and he loved her . . . isn't that sad?'

I was speechless. Vati was only a kitten like me, yet he had so much knowledge. My respect for him grew as I followed him around the lawn.

'Here is an ants' nest,' he said next. 'And the ants told me how frustrated they are because, every time they try to build a mound, a noisy lawnmower comes and chops it off.'

We sat watching the ants scurrying around. One was carrying an egg. I'd never noticed them before.

'Now here, very, very deep down . . . much deeper down than the badger's home . . . is an underground stream . . . it makes the earth tingle,' Vati continued. 'But don't sit there. Underground streams are bad places for cats to be near.'

'How do you know all this?' I asked, amazed.

'It's my gift,' said Vati. He looked deeply into my soul. 'And you know it too. You have only to remember, Timba. You do know because when I was in the cage you sent me a thought along one of the golden roads.'

Later that day Vati wanted to spend time on Angie's lap. Ever so slightly jealous, I stormed out into the evening sunshine to have my usual mad half-hour on my own. I practised belting across the lawn and diving into the bushes that grew along the foot of the wall. The thin bendy branches were good to play with and I did a lot of leaping, catching one between my paws and dragging it down, letting it spring back into the air.

Then I tried again to climb the apple tree the way Vati had climbed it. Halfway up, I was concentrating on turning round safely, when I heard a scratchy whisper. 'Hello, Timba!'

Startled, I dug my claws deeper into the bark and paused, peering round to see where the voice had come from. I meowed, and it came again. 'Timba!'

I looked up, and Leroy was sitting astride the wall under the overhanging foliage. The whites of his eyes shone out from the dark leaves. His trainers were kicking at the stone; he had an open bag in his hand.

'I've come to get you, Timba,' he said in a strange whisper. 'You're MY kitten.'

Chapter Eight

LEROY

'Always welcome him ... with your tail up.'

The words of the Spirit Lion resounded in my head as Leroy and I stared at each other through a whirlpool of decision-making. Vati needed me. I wanted to stay here with Angie and Vati. But my Spirit Lion wanted something else ... and it was unreasonable. I didn't ... did NOT ... want to be Leroy McArthur's cat!

Something had changed in me. I was strong now. I could twist in the air like Vati, and run really fast. My back legs power-boated me across the lawn and through the cat flap with an impressive slam. Eat, I thought, and paused in the kitchen to scoff the remains of Vati's mashed chicken with gravy.

I tried to forget about Leroy, but I was trembling inside. I couldn't forget.

Vati was still on Angie's lap and he gave me a slitty-eyed, blissed-out stare. Angie was asleep with her head on a pink corduroy cushion, and one hand over Vati's sleek back. They looked cosy and peaceful, while I felt stormy and upset.

Leroy was in the garden. He had come for me. What should I do? I'd already done one wrong thing. Now I did something even worse. I was sick on the sofa.

'Oh for goodness' sake, Timba!' Graham shook his newspaper at me. 'Outside.'

Outside was not an option for me. Instead, I sat on the windowsill pretending to wash while Graham fussed around, huffing and sighing, with rolls of paper and disinfectant. The smell gave me a headache. I sat still, hoping he would leave me alone, and he did.

While Angie and Vati went on sleeping, I had a good view of the back garden and the horse field. A small determined figure marched across the field towards a dappled grey pony who raised her head and watched him with interest.

Leroy suddenly looked small and lonely amongst the horses. Angie's horse, Poppy, stood tossing her chestnut head, her tail swishing. I sensed her anxiety as Leroy and the grey pony walked towards each other.

On Saturday mornings I'd watched the children who came to help Angie and Laura with the horses. They spent ages talking to them, brushing them and making friends before riding, and nobody ever rode the grey pony. She was wild, Angie said.

But Leroy didn't know that. He stood close to the pony and got hold of her long mane. Then he vaulted onto her back. For a moment his smile lit up the field. He dug his trainers into the pony's flanks. Her ears went back. She shook herself as if trying to shake him off, then she took off at a gallop with Leroy clinging onto her neck. She headed for a patch of stinging nettles and bucked furiously. Thrown into the air like a rag doll, Leroy crashed into the nettles and lay still.

The excitement fired up the rest of the horses and they joined in the galloping and bucking. The thunder of their hooves woke Angie. 'What's going on?' She quickly put Vati down on the chair and came to the window. 'What's the matter with those horses?'

She watched for a few minutes, but couldn't have seen Leroy. He was lying almost hidden behind the clump of nettles. Only I knew he was there.

'Oh they're just having a gallop round.' Angie sat down again and picked up a book.

I had bonded with Leroy. Now I sensed he was in danger. What should I do? I tried sending Angie a telepathic message. I tried meowing at her. I tried sending her an image of Leroy lying on the ground. She didn't get it.

But Vati did. He jumped up to sit beside me and we both attentively watched the field. Still Leroy didn't move.

The horses lost interest and wandered away, their heads down, munching grass.

It was Angie's horse Poppy who knew what to do. She stared at Leroy and the blaze of light floating towards her. It was coral gold, with streamers of white, and wings that fizzed with energy. Leroy's angel! She looped around the pony and somehow coaxed her to move. Poppy walked carefully towards Leroy, her neck arched and ears pricked as she followed the angel.

She lowered her head and gave Leroy a gentle push with her nose.

'Don't you two kitties want your tea?' Angie called from the kitchen, but Vati and I sat like statues, like the Egyptian cats we had once been, our necks long, our whiskers stiff, our tails neatly curled around ourselves. We were mesmerised by a horse, an angel and a motionless boy.

Poppy lifted her head and turned to face the house. She pawed the ground and whinnied, loud and shrill, an alarm call that soon brought Angie to the window. Poppy saw her and again lowered her head to nudge Leroy with her nose. Then she swung round and once more whinnied at Angie.

'Oh my God! Someone's lying there ... it looks like a child!' Angie gasped, and at the same moment Graham started to 'sing', 'Ah, ah, ah, ah, ah, ah, ah, AH.'

Incensed, Angie tore the music-room door open. 'WILL you stop that bloody singing, Graham, and come and help me. We've got a crisis!'

The sight of Leroy's small body lying on the sofa had a surprising effect on me. I did what the Spirit Lion had told me to do: I went to him with my tail up.

'Here's Timba!' said Angie in a comforting way. She sat at the table nearby, the phone in her hand. 'I don't think it's an emergency,' she said into the phone, 'but we do need a paramedic or a doctor to check him out.'

'Timba!' Leroy smiled for the first time, and his eyes shone. I jumped up and kissed his cold face. He was shivering, and clutching a soft blanket which Graham had put over him. Now Graham was sitting on a stool, close to Leroy, his eyes attentive with concern.

I knew exactly how to stretch myself over Leroy's bony chest and flex my little paws rhythmically. I wanted him to feel the warmth and strength from every part of me ... my soft furry tummy, my paws, my tail ... and, most important, the power of my purring. Once I got it started, it rolled through me like a song from the angels.

'He loves me,' Leroy said in a scratchy whisper, and his eyes filled with tears. 'Did you miss me, Timba?'

'It's OK to cry,' said Graham kindly, and I remembered how loudly Leroy had cried through those long, painful hours in his home. Now his tears ran silently over trembling cheeks. Graham extracted the folded white hanky from his top pocket and gave it to Leroy. He pushed it away. 'I'll make a mess of it,' he said.

'That's what hankies are for,' Graham said, and I noticed his aura was bright, and that Vati had crept up to lie on his shoulder and soak up the healing atmosphere.

'You've got two kittens,' said Leroy.

'This is Vati.'

'Vati! Timba's brother. Timba and Vati.' Leroy smiled again. I went on purring, sensing Vati's approval, giving my whole self to the stream of healing light. Where it came from was no mystery to me. It was woven into the webs of life all over the Planet Earth. I had only to choose a strand from a gold-and-silver thread and let it flow through me. Easy.

'The paramedics are on their way,' said Angie. She sat on the floor by the sofa. 'Aww, look at Timba! He's giving you healing.'

Leroy turned his frightened eyes and looked at Angie.

'I only wanted to see Timba,' he said. 'But he ran indoors, so I went to see the horses.'

'So what happened?'

'I got on that grey to have a ride. I been on a horse before, on a roundabout, but this grey one went mad and chucked me off.'

'She's a young pony. She's never been ridden,' Angie explained. 'She must have been very frightened.'

'I didn't know that, Miss . . . I didn't think horses could be frightened.'

'Why not?'

'Cos they're big.'

'I'm big,' said Graham, 'and I get scared.'

'What are you scared of?' Leroy asked.

'Owls and spooky stuff.'

'I ain't scared of anything,' said Leroy proudly. 'Except my mum.'

'So where is your mum?' Angie asked. 'She's not answering the phone. Do you know her mobile number?'

'She hasn't got a mobile now . . . she got into debt with it.'

'Where is she then, Leroy?'

Leroy shrugged. 'Dunno.'

Angie and Graham looked at each other, and I sensed the telepathy passing between them. Graham frowned. He shook his head ever so slightly, and the bright light drained from his aura. He was going down into a dark confining space, and trying to drag Angie with him. Angie wasn't having it. Nothing fired her passion like negativity and resistance.

'Here are the paramedics.' She pursed her lips, squared her shoulders and went to open the door. Two men in orange came in and Graham picked up Vati and me, one in each hand, and airlifted us into the kitchen.

When the paramedics had gone, we were allowed back in, and Leroy was sitting up looking more like himself.

'I'll take you home in the car,' Angie said.

'No.' Leroy shook his head.

'No? Why not?' asked Angie.

Leroy looked up at her with desolate eyes. 'Mum's not there.'

'So where is she?'

'I dunno.' He shrugged again. 'She left home.'

'What?' Angie looked alarmed. 'Since when?'

'Since . . . I dunno . . . about a week ago.'

'A WEEK! Who's looking after you, Leroy?'

'No one. I got a key . . . and I got half a loaf of bread, and some cornflakes.'

There was a silence. Leroy looked at the floor for a long time. When he raised his eyes they were even more desolate. 'I didn't tell no one, Miss. I don't want to go into care. Can I live with you, Miss? Please . . . I won't be no trouble.'

Angie stared at him. 'Why me?'

'I don't like anyone else.' Leroy's voice was painfully husky. 'Only you ... and Timba. Please, Miss.' He shuffled towards Angie and gave her a hug.

'Oh Leroy! You poor kid.' She hugged him back, and Graham stood with his arms folded, shaking his head and mouthing 'NO' at Angie.

The carefree atmosphere in our home changed from that day, and it was all about Leroy. Angie and Graham talked far into the night, one each end of the sofa, Vati and I blissfully asleep between them. Vati wasn't bothered about what the humans were talking about, but I was. Pretending to be asleep, I listened to snatches of the conversation and felt sure that Angie was winning. I was gunning for her, being her lucky black cat. She talked fast, waving her hands around, and Graham was grunting and sighing. I kept opening one eye to peep at Angie and let her know I was on her side. If only she knew what I knew about Graham ... the secrets he'd often confided to me when he came in late and Angie was in bed.

'I'm glad you can't talk, Timba,' and then he'd tell me about a woman called Lisa and how he couldn't help falling in love with her, and wanted to be with her. 'But Angie must never know. I don't want to lose Angie, or hurt her, Timba. It's our secret, isn't it?' Each time he said that, I'd look still deeper into his soul with my clear golden eyes, and see how his 'secret' was troubling him, and how tightly he was clutching all the threads of his life. I couldn't make him let go. I couldn't change him. All I could do was love him. It's what cats do.

'That was my mother's clock,' he said now, as the clock chimed midnight. 'And she had a big heart ... a heart of gold ... like you, Angie.' He reached across the back of the sofa and touched her hair, moving a curl away from her cheek. 'If Mum was here, she'd want me to say yes.'

I looked at the blaze of light by his left shoulder, and saw within it a lovely old lady, with a face like Graham's, a coil of silver hair, and a smile that warmed the air in a circle around him and Angie. She looked at me kindly, and I gave her a cat smile. Then she waved, and vanished, leaving a glow around us all.

'So ... yes ... OK. Let's give it a go,' Graham said heavily.

Angie leapt to her feet and flung her arms around him. 'I knew you would! Bless you, Graham. It's right. I know it's right.' And she danced round the sofa. 'The Universe has sent us a child!'

Graham smiled, reluctantly, as if his face was out of control. 'Don't get too euphoric,' he warned. 'It won't be easy with young Leroy.'

*

'I can put up with the cats,' Graham said heavily. 'In fact I quite like them. But I can only tolerate THAT BOY in small doses.'

I knew he meant Leroy. Vati and I sat together in our basket, dozing, our eyes half closed, listening to the apparently endless discussions about Leroy. Graham only ever said that to Angie in private. When the 'social workers' came with their sheaves of paper and laptops, and serious faces, Graham pretended to be busy. Or he would shrug and be dismissive. 'Angie and I are not married,' he said now. 'As far as I'm concerned she's free to do whatever she wants. If she wants to foster Leroy, that's fine, but she, not me, is responsible for him.'

'But will you welcome him into your home?'

'I am prepared to,' Graham said. 'I realise Leroy hasn't had a male role model, and I'll do my best. But Angie is the foster parent, not me.'

'He's brilliant with him actually,' Angie said.

'But is your relationship strong?'

Angie and Graham looked at each other.

'Totally,' said Angie, with fire in her eyes. 'We are soul-mates.'

'Hmm.'

Graham maintained an uncomfortable silence, and obviously the social workers didn't 'do' soulmates.

I gave Vati a shove with my nose. The humans were

getting too serious. We jumped out of the basket and confronted each other, making terrible fish faces and pretending we were deadly enemies. Vati arched his back, leaped sideways and embarked on a wild, rug-crunching challenge with me trying to catch him, then hiding and trying to head him off. When I pounced out at him, we collided in mid-air with our paws wide open like flowers.

Angie laughed, but no matter what we kittens did, Graham's mouth just twitched, the social workers stayed po-faced, and the talking droned relentlessly on.

Eventually I jumped onto Angie's lap and tried to calm her down. She was trying too hard, and I sensed it. To me she seemed like the only person in the room who was truly alive. Her passionate words were beating against a wall of resistance, and finally she lost her temper.

'We are talking about an abandoned child,' she stormed, and I felt the heat from her aura and the drumbeat of her heart under my fur. 'Why make it so complicated? Leroy's mother has abandoned him. He needs a home ... NOW ... not in six months' time ... and he wants to be with me. He's made that perfectly clear. I've made my offer to be his foster mum ... and it's a good offer, so let's stop nit-picking and make a decision for the sake of this child's emotional well-being.'

Vati climbed the bookshelves and sat up there disapprovingly, like he always did if there was a row. He told me he was getting clear of the bad energy, sitting close to the ceiling.

I stayed with Angie. Her fire had never hurt me, and it didn't now. 'Bless you, Timba,' she whispered into my fur, as the social worker snapped her laptop closed and stood up.

'I hear what you're saying, Angie,' she said with infuriating calm. 'We will make an assessment and let you know. Until then, Leroy can spend Saturdays with you. We'll bring him out.'

When they had gone, Angie marched around, imitating the social workers. 'Make an assessment!' she raged. 'Meanwhile that boy is desperate. Ooh, I wish I could KIDNAP him.'

Chapter Nine

THE STRUGGLE

Vati spent most of his quiet time with Graham, who seemed bewitched by the attention from the elegant little cat. Vati waited until Graham was sprawled in a chair, and then walked gracefully up his arms, round his neck and shoulders, nibbling his ears and kissing his face. He usually ended up spreadeagled across Graham's vast chest, being rocked gently by his breathing. Once Vati followed him into the music room with his tail up, and got away with walking along the keyboard. But then he sharpened his claws on the furniture and Graham shouted at him. 'Stop that, Vati. NO.' But Vati coolly went on doing it until he was satisfied. Graham tried to chase him, but Vati just sat there and looked up at him beguilingly, and in the end Graham picked him up, sighing. 'We'll have to find a way of stopping you doing that,' he said.

Vati didn't like Leroy, and when the boy came in on Saturday morning, and tried to pick him up, Vati used those sharp claws to scratch his hands.

'Ow!' Leroy looked at the beads of blood emerging from his skin, and Vati sat washing himself as if to cleanse all trace of Leroy from his fur.

'He's different from Timba,' Angie said as she rubbed some cream on Leroy's scratches. 'Timba is tolerant. Vati is a hypersensitive cat. If you want to pick him up, you must ask permission.'

'But how do you know whether he says yes or no?' Leroy asked, frowning.

'Well, he said NO very clearly, by scratching you,' said Angie. 'But it doesn't have to come to that. A cat wouldn't come over and scratch you for nothing, Leroy. So you have to approach him gently, and sense if he wants contact with you . . . and if he doesn't, then you leave him alone.'

Leroy didn't look convinced.

'You wouldn't like some giant to come and grab you and lift you up into the air, would you?' said Angie.

'I'd fight him.' Leroy raised his fists. 'Wham!'

'Well that's what Vati did. He's teaching you.'

'He's not a teacher! He's a cat.'

'Cats are great teachers ... and so are horses.' Angie had a way of making her eyes sparkle with excitement when she was telling children something. Her eyes held Leroy mesmerised.

'But they can't talk,' he said. 'Teachers have to talk, don't they?'

Angie shut her mouth and shook her head. Still looking at him, she picked up a rope from the pile of horse harnesses that was lying in the kitchen, and tried to give Leroy a silent demonstration of how to tie a knot. He ended up giggling, and so did she.

I loved to hear humans laughing. It fired me up like nothing else. I charged across the floor and pounced on a horse harness, getting it in a tangle, and making Vati leap in the air like a grasshopper. The house rang with laughter.

Only Graham was silent, skulking behind a crackly newspaper which was covered in gloom. The soles of his feet twitched as if he was annoyed by the fun rampaging through his house ... and it was his house, not Angie's house, as he frequently reminded us.

The long hot summer was a happy time for Vati and me. We were young cats now, almost fully grown. Everyone admired me, and that helped me to become loving and confident. I loved it when Graham looked at me and said, 'That cat is really chocolate box.'

119

Angie spent a lot of time patiently teaching Leroy how to talk to me, how to hold me kindly, and how to tune in to my needs. He seemed like a different boy, the boy he wanted to be. On his weekly visits I never heard him cry, and all the time his eyes were wide open with wonder at the new things he was discovering.

Graham refused to take much interest in Leroy, until one wet Saturday when Leroy sidled up to him with a book in his hand. 'Will you read me a story?' he asked.

'Ask Angie,' Graham said.

'She's getting lunch,' said Leroy, and stood looking at Graham beguilingly. 'Please.'

I decided to get in on the act and jumped onto Graham's lap to soften the hard shell he was trying to maintain. A stare from my golden eyes and a silent meow soon had him sighing and reluctantly taking the book. 'Aren't you a bit old to have stories read to you?'

Leroy looked disappointed. 'But I like your voice,' he said. 'It makes the story come real and Timba wants a story too, don't you, Timba?'

Graham gave in and started to read with Leroy sitting on the arm of the chair, his eyes wide and inquisitive, and me purring on his lap. It soon became obvious that Graham was enjoying it as much as Leroy. Even Vati wanted to be part of it, and he draped himself over Graham's shoulder from where he could see the pictures in the book and feel the rumble of Graham's voice.

I sensed the angels, and basked in the warm, smooth glow they were building around us, binding us together, wanting us to be a family. But Graham was still harbouring that secret in his eyes, and when I stared into them it was a shadow dancing, waiting for its time.

On another Saturday, Vati and I were sitting in the sun on the hot stony slabs beside the pond. Vati was completely absorbed by something. Now and again he twitched his tail and stretched his neck, as if whatever he was watching had moved.

'What are you looking at?' I asked.

Vati ignored me. He was too intent. So I moved round and peeped at his eyes. They glinted green with a mystic sparkle which I loved to see. Vati seemed to be twice as alive as me.

'I'm witnessing a struggle,' he said. Following his gaze I saw an ugly, crusty-looking creature clinging to a reed. It seemed to be stuck with its head in some kind of tight casing, its sectioned body arched, straining to free itself. It had a rhythm of struggling and resting, struggling and resting, and nothing much changed. I got bored watching it, but Vati didn't. 'I'm tuning in to this being,' he said. 'It's desperate to fly free before the sun goes down.

I think it's going to be beautiful, and I want to give it to Graham to show how much I love him.'

'What you looking at, Timba?' Leroy sat himself down next to us. He'd learned from Angie and the horses that he had to approach animals quietly, not at full throttle, so when he arrived, neither of us moved. I did grant him a muted purr-meow and a sidelong cat smile.

His self-control vanished when he saw the creature heave and twitch to escape from its shell. Leroy jumped to his feet and pounded towards the house. 'Angie! ANGIE ... quick, there's a THING in the pond,' he shouted.

'It won't be there much longer if you shout like that,' Angie said as she emerged, drying her hands on her jeans.

'Quick ... quick! It might be an ALIEN,' whispered Leroy, and the garden rang with Angie's laughter.

'Don't touch it,' she said firmly.

I sensed that Angie was stressed, despite the laughter. Earlier, she and Graham had been arguing about why he was always home late. As soon as the car turned in and Leroy's 'social worker' brought him to the door, the argument had stopped and hung in the air like a hostile rain cloud. Nothing had been resolved, and I'd done my best, walking to and fro between them, trying to coax a spark of forgiveness. When Leroy came, Graham spoke to him briefly, then took his laptop to the music room.

Angie pasted on a smile and pretended she was happy.

We cats see it all.

The four of us sat watching 'the thing' still struggling on the reed. A beam of sunlight touched the curve of its scaly body with a glint of brightest blue. It heaved, then stopped and kept still.

'Is it dead?' Leroy whispered.

'Probably not,' said Angie.

Leroy started to take his shoes off. 'I'm gonna paddle in there and help it get out.'

'NO!' Angie looked fierce enough to make Leroy freeze with one shoe in his hand.

'Why not?' he asked.

'Because . . . it's the struggle that makes it strong,' Angie said, and as she spoke the creature gave a final heave and the rest of its body popped out and straightened into a tail of iridescent turquoise. Two glistening wings slowly spread out to dry in the sun. Leroy gasped. 'A dragonfly! It's massive.'

The dragonfly turned its complex eyes and looked at us with luminous wisdom.

'Hello, dragonfly,' said Leroy. His smile beamed round the garden and his aura flared with light. 'Can you fly now?'

I meowed to encourage the beautiful creature, and Vati's eyes flashed green in the sun, the tip of his tail twitching. But Angie looked unexpectedly sad. I ran to her and rubbed myself against her. In the deep heart of her mind a pain was rising. I could feel its unstoppable power.

Something was wrong with Angie.

'You stay and watch it fly away,' she said quietly to Leroy. 'But don't touch it. Promise?'

'Promise.' Leroy beamed and banged his hand against hers.

Angie tried to smile but her face was stiff. She stood up and walked slowly back to the house, her arms wrapped tightly around herself. I ran beside her with my tail up, and she was repeating and repeating the words: 'It's the struggle that makes it strong.'

For once she didn't pick me up for a cuddle. I sat on the windowsill and watched over her, offering the odd fragment of a purr, as she whizzed around the kitchen chopping vegetables and scooping them into a pan. Her aura was unusually dark, and her eyes joyless. She didn't want to stop and look at me, and I figured it was because she knew that I knew. Talking about it, even to me, would be too painful.

Moments later a harrowing sound rang through the garden. Leroy was crying, louder than ever before. I peeped out and he was lying face down on the lawn, beating the earth with his fists. And Vati was padding proudly through the kitchen with the dragonfly hanging, broken, from his mouth. Resolutely he headed through the open door of the music room with his precious gift for Graham.

The singing stopped. Graham's nose and mouth curled in disgust as he saw Vati's gift lying by his shoe. At arm's length he picked up the broken dragonfly by one of its glassy wings. 'Yuk!' Snarling, he crossed the room and held it high up above the trash can, which was a shiny tin with music notes painted on it. Graham dropped the dragonfly in there, and we heard the ping as it landed. 'You horrible cat!' he growled at Vati. I winced. Vati's eyes filled with shock and pain. Running low and scared, he streaked out of the music room, his tail down, his eyes dark and frowning.

I followed Vati to the edge of the horse field and found him crouched inside an old barrel that was on its side in the hedge. He was devastated.

'I'm not going back,' he said. 'I took Graham the nicest gift, the best thing I've ever caught, and he called me a horrible cat. And Leroy wants to kill me. What is it with humans?'

There were no words to comfort him, so I kissed his face and licked him, purring and caring. He soaked it up in silence, but he wouldn't come back to the house with me.

'I want to spend time with the moon and the stars,' he said, and looked towards the blue hills far away across the fields.

'This isn't a very nice place to sit,' I remarked, sniffing at the dirty old barrel he had used as a haven.

'Oh ... but it is,' Vati said. 'Open your eyes, Timba. This barrel is on a sacred node point where two of the golden lines intersect. Surely you can feel it?'

I couldn't.

'It energises me to sit here,' Vati said. 'If you want to listen to your Spirit Lion, you should come here and it will be easy for you.'

'So what's wrong with Graham?' I asked.

'He is trapped, like the dragonfly was, and struggling to get free.'

Leroy cried for hours over the dragonfly. To him it was a tragedy, to Vati it was a triumph and a perfect gift. To Graham it was something horrible.

Angie took the crying Leroy back out into the garden. She opened the shed, and he peered in. 'We're going to do something AMAZING,' she said, and put a spade into his hand. 'You carry that.'

I followed them with my tail up into the vegetable garden, where I sat watching. I wanted to learn how Angie would stop Leroy crying so much. 'I know it's sad,' she said, 'but we've done enough crying, don't you think?'

Leroy shook his head miserably.

'Well I'm going to move on,' said Angie, 'otherwise I'll miss out on some of the other miracles happening in the garden. Now ... do you remember what we buried in the ground, Leroy? Ages ago, in the spring?'

His eyes brightened. 'A potato,' he said huskily. I ran to him and rubbed my fur against his bare legs, purring, trying to coax him out of his grief.

'Well, now we're going to dig down and see what's happened to it. Who's going to dig?'

'Me. Let me!'

Leroy dug eagerly, flinging earth across the garden like a dog digging. I darted out of the way, flicking my tail, and sat up on a pile of wood to watch. I worried in case Leroy dug up the sleeping badger.

Angie helped him loosen the potato plant, easing it out in a shower of earth. From its roots hung a bunch of creamy white new potatoes. Leroy gasped. His mouth and eyes opened in astonishment. He scooped up the baby potatoes and dropped them into a bucket. 'FIFTEEN!' he shouted, and his radiance lit up the garden. 'We got fifteen potatoes.'

'There's the old one ...' Angie showed him the dusty old potato in the middle of it all. 'And there's more ... look!'

Together they scrabbled in the earth like two rabbits.

'It's like buried treasure.' Leroy grinned happily, his hands covered in soil, his eyes shining. 'I didn't know you could get potatoes out of the ground.'

'Shall we cook them?' said Angie. 'Quick, help me before Graham goes out. We'll have new potatoes with butter.'

'New potatoes with butter,' repeated Leroy.

'You're strong. You carry the bucket.'

Leroy set off, proudly, the bucket clanking in his hand. 'New potatoes with butter,' he sang, and the three of us headed for the kitchen, me with my tail up.

Angie was definitely an earth-angel, I thought, and almost believed I saw the shimmer of her wings. But what had Poppy meant when she said, 'Earth-angels always take on more than they can manage'?

Chapter Ten

PURE CELESTIAL ENERGY

It seemed a long time to me before Angie finally got what she wanted. Vati and I were cats now and we had lived through our first autumn and winter. Our coats were glossy, and we were beautiful and strong. The only bad time was when Angie took us to the vet to have us 'done'! 'Sorry, guys,' she explained. 'But it's better for you long-term, and better for the Planet. We don't want you making hordes of unwanted kittens.' Rick was gentle with us, and we went to sleep together and woke up together, and got safely home in the luxurious travelling basket Angie had bought us.

When the blossom was on the apple tree and the bees humming in the spring sunshine, the social workers finally allowed Leroy to come and live with us. I supervised while Angie set up a bedroom for him with a cosy bed. She put posters on the walls, and bought him a blanket with lions on it. He had a brightly coloured beanbag, which I loved, and a bookshelf, and boxes of stuff which I remembered from his home. Even the old teddies were there, freshly washed and pleased with themselves.

The only thing Leroy wanted when he arrived was me. He seemed awed by the majestic cat I had grown into.

The other thing Leroy wanted to do was climb the apple tree, and we did that together, Vati and I showing off as we led him up through the branches. When he'd done it once, Leroy called out to Angie, 'I climbed the flower tree.'

'The flower tree?' Angie came out into the garden, looking puzzled.

'That one,' said Leroy, pointing to the apple tree.

'Oh . . . that's an apple tree!' Angie said, her voice kind.

'No it's not,' Leroy grinned. 'It hasn't got apples on it . . . it's a flower tree.'

Angie smiled at him. 'You come and look at this, and I'll tell you a secret.' She held one of the blossoms still for him. 'See that little blob in the middle of the flower?'

'Yeah.' Leroy frowned.

'THAT,' said Angie, 'will turn into an apple.'

'No it won't.' Leroy rolled his eyes incredulously.

'It takes all summer,' said Angie. 'The petals fall off and that little green blob swells up like a balloon and becomes an apple.'

'You're kidding!'

'No, it's true. You'll see it happen. In a few weeks the flowers will have gone and you'll see tiny green apples, too small to eat. BUT . . . ' Angie widened her eyes even more, and Leroy looked mesmerised. 'It won't happen unless a bee goes into the flower. There's one . . . look. Let's watch it and see what it's doing.'

'It might come out and sting you.'

'No it won't, it's too busy pollinating.'

'Pollinating,' repeated Leroy. 'Are you joking, Angie?'

'No.'

Leroy didn't look convinced. 'Well, Mum got her apples from Tesco,' he said. 'She didn't get them off a tree.'

At night Leroy's bedroom door was left open so that I could go in and lie close to him, purring, as he slept.

One night he didn't go to sleep, but lay there talking to me. 'My mum didn't want me, Timba. She left me alone in the house and the social workers took me into care. They wouldn't listen when I said I wanted to live with Angie. That's why I missed playing with you when you were a kitten, but I still love you now you're big.'

He got up and put the light on. Then he roamed

around the room in his bare feet, a box of pens in his hand. I watched anxiously. I knew what he was going to do!

The walls in Leroy's bedroom were covered in posters, and he couldn't find a space. He drifted out onto the landing and listened with his ear to the closed door of Angie and Graham's room. He turned and gave me a thumbs-up and a beaming smile. 'They're asleep,' he said in a stage whisper. He switched the lights on and surveyed the pale green bare wall along the landing, took the lid off a pen, and began to draw. First he did a pair of hypnotic yellow eyes. I watched anxiously, my tail twitching, as he drew with swift, skilful strokes, and the rest of the lion appeared on the wall.

A fox was barking out in the night, and the wind blew scatters of rain against the window. Leroy worked on, in a silent frenzy. I felt as if that lion was in the house, drawing its own picture through the wildly moving arm of a pyjama-clad boy.

I knew that in the morning Leroy would be in terrible trouble. I wanted him to stop. An ordinary meow had no effect, except that Leroy put his finger to his lips and whispered, 'Shh, Timba. We gotta be quiet. I'll draw the curly mane now . . . in colours!' And he worked furiously, doing crinkling lines around the lion's face. His pens fell to the floor, the white tops rolling everywhere, and I couldn't resist playing with them, batting them through the banisters to the hall floor below.

Vati sensed the excitement and came trotting upstairs. He slunk up to Leroy's lion, and peered at its eyes, and dismissed it as unimportant. We played with the pen tops, filling the silent house with whirrs and clicks and the muffled thud of paws belting up and down the stairs.

The dawn chorus was starting when Leroy decided the lion was finished. He stood back to look at it with a satisfied smile. Leaving the pens scattered on the floor, he went back to bed, and the house fell silent.

I followed Vati downstairs and out through the cat flap into the light of the rising sun. We caught a mouse each and took them back into the house to play with. I ate mine, but Vati chucked his on top of the piano and left it there for Graham. He went straight to sleep in our favourite armchair, while I stayed awake, washing and listening. I was nervous about what Leroy had done. I wanted to warn Angie before Graham woke up. I felt it justified an amplified extended-meow, so I sat outside her bedroom door and did one, a real beauty. Then I stuck my claws out and tapped on the door, politely, like a human.

I heard a groan and a yawn. Graham opened the door. 'What's up, Timba?' I looked around at the scattered pens and the lion on the wall and felt it was my fault.

Leroy appeared, and he didn't look nervous at all. His

eyes danced with excitement. 'You like my lion?' he said to Graham. 'It's a surprise.'

In one of Leroy's story books was a picture of a very hairy, very angry giant towering over a downtrodden little farmer. Graham looked exactly like that giant as he stood there in his boxers, staring open-mouthed at Leroy's lion. I saw a red flash burn upwards through his aura until it reached his head and Graham pushed his fingers through his hair and made it wild and scraggy.

The smile was disappearing from Leroy's face, and the silence hung in the air. I felt it reaching into my memory, and I recalled the time in my early kittenhood when a man had shouted, and instantly extinguished any spiritual light. I didn't want Graham to shout at Leroy and destroy the bright joy in the boy's heart.

So I did another amplified extended-meow and gave Graham a stare that he couldn't ignore. It helped him with the rage he was struggling to control.

'You angry?' whispered Leroy.

Graham raised his eyebrows and made his voice quiet. He sat down on the wide window seat. 'Come here, Leroy. I need to explain something to you.'

Leroy shuffled over to him.

'Look at me, please,' Graham said, and his own eyes were so full of light that Leroy looked at him attentively, seeming fascinated by this giant of a man who could speak quietly when he was angry. Graham used that same hushed tone to create suspense when he was reading stories to Leroy.

'This is my house,' Graham said. 'And I like it, in fact, I love it. I lived here when I was a little boy, like you. I like it to look clean and bright, and if I want a picture, I put it in a nice frame, with glass over it, like that one there.' He pointed to a nearby painting of the sea. 'It looks good, doesn't it?'

Leroy grunted. 'Yeah.' He fidgeted and I could see he was still expecting Graham to shout at him the way Janine had done.

'So . . . I'll tell you what we are going to do about that lion that's appeared on the wall . . . look at me, Leroy,' Graham continued. 'I must say . . . it's a quality drawing . . . very good. BUT.' His voice rose slightly. 'I don't want it on our nice clean wall. So, what I'm going to do is take a photo of it with my digital camera, and you can help me make a posh frame for it . . . then we can hang it on the wall. We can even put it on Facebook.' Leroy's smile was reappearing, only to vanish as Graham spoke, low and sinister. 'However . . . I am going out after breakfast, until lunchtime, and when I come back I want to see that wall painted a nice apple green like it was before. Otherwise the photo will stay inside my camera. Do you understand, Leroy?'

'Yeah.'

'AND . . . ' The red flash burnt through Graham's aura again. 'Look at me. I want a promise that you'll never, never, never EVER draw on my wall in my house again.'

'OK,' Leroy mumbled.

'Is that a deal?'

'Deal.' Leroy banged his small hand against Graham's giant one.

'But . . . we'll put my lion on FACEBOOK?'

'We'll put the lion on Facebook,' Graham promised, and Vati came running upstairs with his tail up, and made a fuss of Graham, purring and gazing adoringly at him. Cats like quiet voices too.

Later, Angie covered the floor with a sheet and set Leroy up with a tin of apple green paint and a roller. Painting over his lion made him cry, but he got on with it, and made a mess. His hair and his hands were smeared with paint, and there were drips everywhere.

'Keep those cats away from the wet paint,' Angie said. 'We don't want two apple green cats!'

Too late. Vati and I had already played around on the slippery sheet. Vati had trodden in one of the drips and left apple green paw marks along the landing and down the stairs. And I had managed to sit in a pool of paint.

'Timba's got an apple green bum,' said Angie, laughing. 'Oh dear . . . I'll have to bath you, Timba,' and I had to endure being 'encouraged' to sit in a bowl of warm water and let her slosh it over my fur.

The day ended with supper in the garden, blackbirds singing and petals from the apple blossom drifting around us. We were family, sharing ups and downs and growing closer. But only I knew the secret that haunted Graham's mind.

The trouble between Angie and Graham came to a head in the autumn.

Vati led me into ever more daring escapades. He would scale the wire around the chicken pen and jump down onto the roof of the wooden chicken house. Then he'd sit there coolly observing the hens, while I sat sensibly outside the pen, looking in.

I was on a polite nose-to-beak relationship with the cockerel, strictly through the wire, and not too often. Just common courtesy and respect. But Vati really pushed his luck, and one day the cockerel flew at him with his colours blazing. I would have retaliated, but Vati simply rolled onto his back and waved his paws in the air. The sight of his sleek tummy and shining black pads seemed to disarm the outraged cockerel who turned and stalked off.

'I'm a peacemaker,' Vati often told me. He'd actually made friends with Leroy, allowing a tentative stroking session, and the occasional cuddle, strictly on Vati's terms.

I wished Vati could make peace between Angie and Graham. There were more and more times when Graham came home late, and one day when Angie was at work and Leroy at school, he brought a woman friend into our home. Her name was Lisa, and she didn't like cats. Especially me.

'I couldn't stand a cat like him,' she said to Graham. 'Look at the fluff he leaves everywhere. I don't mind the other little cat. Vati, is it? He's kind of cute.'

I felt hurt. I didn't deliberately leave my fur around the place! Eat, I thought, and retreated to my bowl where I tucked into my generous portion of 'rabbit with tuna'.

'And look at the size of him,' Lisa said scathingly. 'I bet he is a really greedy cat.'

When I started on Vati's meal, Graham came and whipped the dish away. 'That's Vati's food, you greedy cat,' he said. I lashed my tail, and glared at him. It wasn't like Graham to insult me. We were buddies, weren't we?

I wanted Vati to curl up with me, and calm me down, but he went swanning into the music room with Graham and Lisa. The singing began, and Lisa had a high soprano voice like a cat. I resented her. How dare she criticise ME when she was the fattest human I'd ever seen. Her tummy stuck right out, nearly touching the piano as she sang, balanced precariously on two slim legs and a pair of sparkly gold sandals.

Something felt wrong. When the singing stopped Graham knelt on the floor in front of Lisa and leaned his head against her fat tummy. 'How's the little person in there?' he asked.

'She's fine.' Lisa patted her tummy. 'She was moving around when we were singing. She likes music!'

I curled up, alone in my basket, wishing Angie and Leroy would come home, wishing I could go to sleep and shut out the sound of Lisa and Graham. They sat on the sofa, cuddling and talking quietly. Betrayal, I thought angrily. Couldn't Vati see it?

The gift of sleep eluded me as I watched them discreetly with my eyes half open. I definitely didn't feel like purring, but I could hear Vati's economical little purr as he seduced Graham, lying on his shoulder like a drape of silk. Soon Vati was deeply asleep, leaving me to listen in horror to the conversation.

'I'm not going to share a house with HER,' Lisa said. And I understood that the loud 'HER' meant my beloved Angie.

'Of course not, darling. She'll have to go,' said Graham. 'Damn it, this is my house. I inherited it from my parents ... I was an only child. I grew up here... can't imagine living anywhere else. Oh yes ... Angie will have to go ... and her chickens, and THAT BOY she is insisting on fostering.' Graham frowned, still smoothing Vati's

139

silken coat with one hand. 'And the cats . . . but I might keep this little fellow.'

'Have you told Angie yet?' Lisa asked.

'No,' Graham said heavily. 'I will, when the time is right.'

'You said that last time.'

'Sure . . . I did. But it is not a task I relish, Lisa. Angie is very volatile. She'll fly into a rage. I dread it . . . and, if I'm honest, I don't know how best to tell her.'

'You'll have to grasp the nettle. You're not married.'

'No.' Graham sighed and fidgeted.

'So when are you going to tell her, Graham?'

'I wish I didn't have to.'

'Do you still love her?'

'No.' Graham looked defensive. 'But I don't want to hurt her. She's stressed enough with Leroy and the teaching job. I should at least wait until the end of term.'

'That will be Christmas. You can't chuck her out on Christmas Eve, Graham. Even I know that!'

'Can we put this discussion on hold, please?' Graham pleaded. 'Let's focus on the concerts.' He held up his hand as Lisa tried to protest. 'I promise I will tell Angie, in the fullness of time.'

Devastated, I slunk out of the house, feeling I couldn't bear to stay in there. Angie had promised me a 'for-ever home', and Vati. What was going to happen? The conversation hung over me, and the words swerved and twisted in my mind. 'Angie will have to go ... and her chickens, and THAT BOY ... and the cats.'

It was unthinkable.

I headed for my magic place, the circle of stones on the back lawn. Thick grey clouds were piling in from the west, and the wind ruffled my fur. I couldn't get comfortable. Driven by the need for total stillness and shelter, I trotted across the lawn and found the barrel Vati had used. A node point, he'd said, a place of enchantment where the golden roads crossed. Right now I needed something like that.

I heard the sounds of Graham taking THAT LISA home in his car. I wondered where Vati was. I needed him.

But I stayed in the barrel, and felt nothing except anxiety and the chill of autumn.

Then I heard Angie and Leroy arriving, Leroy's feet thundering around the place as he looked for me. 'Timba. Timba, where are you?'

I stayed hidden.

Cats shouldn't have to worry about humans, I thought, as I waited for the Spirit Lion. He came wrapped in white light, his eyes peaceful and amused. He coaxed me out of the barrel, and the sky had cleared. Pale and warm, the afternoon sun seemed to arrive with the Lion, even though it was autumn.

'You're a fine cat, Timba,' he said as I settled down between his pillow-soft paws.

'But what's going to happen to me?' I asked, and the whole problem suddenly magnified in my mind. Where would Angie take us? How far away? I loved our home at Graham's. Vati and I knew every corner, every wall and every tree. We knew where the sun rose and where to shelter from the wind. We had friends here, good friends like Poppy and Laura, and the heron who came to the pond. I couldn't imagine living somewhere else. This was home.

'You will be strong enough for everything you need to do, Timba,' he said reassuringly. 'Angie will take care of you and Vati. Don't worry about places . . . wherever you are on this special Planet, you have lines of communication, and when you go on a journey, you can follow the golden roads.'

'How can I find a golden road?' I asked.

'I'll teach you how to find one.' The Lion closed his eyes. 'Be very still, and close your eyes with me. Then you'll be able to see so much more. Do this, always, when you are lost. And don't tuck your paws up like that. Your pads are very sensitive. Use them,' he continued as I quickly rearranged myself. 'When your pads are touching the earth they will pick up information ... and when you feel the buzz and see the gold in your mind, then you are on a golden road. Keep your eyes closed ... for when they are open your finer senses are weakened.'

I thought about my paws, and the way they felt on the damp earth. My pads began to detect a buzzy sensation, as if I was touching a bumblebee. It was coming from deep under the earth, and it wasn't confined to one spot, it was travelling in a limitless flowing stream. It wasn't water. It wasn't fire.

'What is it?' I asked the Spirit Lion.

'Pure celestial energy,' he said, 'such as you had in the spirit world, Timba. Don't you remember?'

'No,' I said.

'The memory is there ... in your mind ... somewhere,' said the Spirit Lion, and his voice deepened. 'Before you were born into this life, you crossed the river of forget-fulness, and for you that was a powerful block. You were intended to be a brave and loving cat, a leader, a real Earth cat ... a support cat.'

'A support cat?' I queried.

'A cat who is so important that a human cannot live without you. And I think you know who that human is, Timba.'

'Leroy.' I couldn't hide my disappointment. 'But I wish it was Angie.'

'Angie is your earth–angel. She loves you, but she's not dependent on you. Leroy is. You are the first soul on Earth to offer him unconditional love.'

'I am?'

The thought was so awesome that we both sank into silence, a nurturing, creative silence that drifted into purring. I felt the Spirit Lion melting away like a cloud of steam vanishing into the landscape . . . still there, but gone!

I focused on what he had told me, closing my eyes and keeping my pads on the earth to feel the 'pure celestial energy'. Vati knows about that, I realised, and the instant I thought about him, my beautiful, poetic brother came gliding through the long grass to find me.

'You need to lighten up, Timba,' he said. His eyes sparkled with mischief. He dived into the barrel and went mad in there with sticks and straw, making explosive rustlings. Then he pounced on me, leapt in the air and challenged me to a wrestling match. We lashed our tails and made faces at each other, then rolled on the floor in a tangle of pedalling paws. The excitement sent us flying around the garden with me chasing Vati, both of us on fire with joy.

What would I do without my amazing brother?

Chapter Eleven

THE SCREAM OF AN ANGEL

Christmas passed in a comfortable haze of fairy lights and plates of turkey. Angie made us a playhouse from a big cardboard box, and we were given a new catnip mouse each. We experienced the frosty garden and came in with our fur ruffed out and diamond drops on our whiskers. Angie laughed a lot and took funny photographs of Vati and me warming our bellies in the glow of the wood burner. Happy cats.

I loved the winking fairy lights, and I enjoyed watching Leroy tearing the paper off his presents. Inside one parcel was a sleek silver laptop, and that was the first time I ever heard Leroy say 'thank you' with a look of pure wonder in his eyes. He seemed overwhelmed and sat on the floor staring at his presents, while Vati and I crunched the torn paper and skidded around. It was pure happiness.

The Spirit Lion tried to warn me that things could change. 'Christmas is a strange time for humans,' he said. 'It's too much artificial happiness and it collapses into a black hole.'

Two days later, I found out what he meant.

Leroy had gone out for the day with his social worker to see his mum. Janine had been found living in a distant town, and she had agreed to see Leroy regularly, with his social worker. The visits disturbed Leroy, and he would come home moody and sad. As soon as Leroy had left, Graham handed Angie a letter. He looked guilty, like a dog who had dug a hole in the lawn.

'What's this?' Angie sat down on the sofa and unfolded the white paper. Graham stood over her, fidgeting, and I sensed his heart thumping too fast in that huge chest.

A strange light came into Vati's eyes, lemon bright and suspicious. Sensing trouble, he immediately climbed to the top of the bookshelves, and sat up there, hunched and attentive. I rolled on the rug and couldn't be bothered to move.

An icy silence chilled our happy room. I turned to watch Angie. Her aura was sparking, and there was a sense that time had stopped in the air above a chasm. Her thoughts were spinning. She grasped the arm of the sofa and stuttered out some words. 'You can't do this to me, Graham.'

Graham stood there like a teddy bear, his eyes fixed and glassy, his fingers and thumb pulling at his collar.

Angie's skin flushed crimson.

'It's my house, Angie. We're not married,' said Graham quietly.

'You BASTARD!' Angie leapt to her feet and screamed in a way I would never forget. The scream of an angel is the most harrowing sound on Earth.

Shaken to the edges of my fur, I quickly jumped up to sit in the window, behind the velvet curtain. The glass was cold, and the winter wind whipped across the garden, blowing hard beads of snow.

'All the LOVE I've put into this place.' Angie's words flew at Graham like wasps. 'The WORK I've done. It was bleak when I came here. Graham, you've used me. You've betrayed me. And who is this bloody woman?' Her voice shattered into another scream, her hands clenching at her hair.

'Please don't swear,' said Graham coldly, 'and her name is Lisa.' He flicked his mobile phone. 'There's a photo of her here, look . . . it's a nice one. She's a sweet girl, you'd like her.'

'Like her?' Angie jumped to her feet and tore Graham's letter into flakes that fell like snow onto the carpet.

The row raged on and on. I only caught fragments of it as I hid behind the curtain looking out at the snow. I glanced at Vati and he'd obviously seen it too. We made a telepathic agreement to inspect it later.

'And what about Leroy?' Angie said. She looked at Graham with fierce, hot eyes. 'All that stuff I've been through with the social workers, fighting for him, fighting to get full-time foster care ... and just when he's settling down ... you pull the rug out!'

'Everything I have to say is in that letter,' Graham said. 'You'd better piece it together and read it. Or open your laptop. I took the precaution of putting it in an email too. I'm not going to stand here arguing. I've got a rehearsal.'

'Oh go on ... walk away!' Angie screamed. 'You heartless, devious BASTARD!'

Graham stalked out and shut the door. Moments later we heard his car pulling into the lane. I watched its red lights disappear into the whirling snow.

I ran to Angie who had crumpled onto the sofa. She seemed numb with shock. 'Oh Timba! Dear darling, lovely cat.' She cried into my fur, and I felt the gratitude she was sending me through her pain. I leaned against her heart and spread myself right out, wanting to give her all my warmth, my loudest purr, my long soft paws reaching up to pat her burning face. I almost couldn't bear her pain. It was hard for me to stay there, but I knew I had to. A frenzy of snowflakes hit the window. I wanted to play, and just be a cat.

Angie picked up the phone. 'Can you come round, Laura? . . . please . . . I've had a devastating shock.'

Minutes later, Laura was there, shaking the snow from her coat. She took her boots off and came to sit with Angie on the sofa. 'My God, you look terrible, Angie. What's happened?'

There was a brief silence, and then Angie really let go of her feelings, almost shaking me off her lap. I pretended not to notice and went on purring.

'Graham . . . the love of my life . . . is chucking me out.'

'WHAT? He can't do that, Angie!'

'He's got some other PIG of a woman.' Angie wept bitterly. 'How I hate her. Lisa, she's called . . . and she's everything I'm not. A singer, with a face like a Barbie doll . . . oh he had the cheek to show me a photo of her, would you believe?'

'How insensitive. That's so cruel.' Laura sat with her arms around Angie, her eyes full of caring love.

'And she's such a good little home-maker . . . cup cakes and shiny gadgets,' stormed Angie, 'and, wouldn't you know it . . . she's pregnant as well . . . oh God, that's hurt me more than anything, Laura. I SO wanted a baby, and I kept miscarrying, and . . . it broke my heart. Three times. It's so unfair. What have I done to deserve this? Tell me that, Laura.'

'Nothing,' Laura said fiercely. 'You've been brilliant, Angie. You're a fantastic friend . . . and look what you've done here. This place was a tip.'

'I've worked so hard. I put everything into the relationship. Graham never notices . . . and when I lost those darling babies, he . . . he just expected me to go on as if nothing had happened . . . and I tried . . . oh God how I tried. No one knows. Maybe I should have been miserable . . . but that's not me. I'm a positive person. Why has this happened to me? WHY?' Angie was now so distressed that her voice was high-pitched and croaky.

'Don't torment yourself with the WHY stuff, Angie. Life is just so cruel sometimes.'

'It's not life. It's HIM.'

'Is that his letter on the floor in bits?' asked Laura.

Angie stood up. 'Can you hold Timba?' she asked and I was put on Laura's lap which smelled of horses. 'He's sent it by email too.' She opened her laptop and the screen flickered into life. 'I mean . . . read it, Laura.'

'Haven't got my glasses,' Laura said.

'I'll read it to you then.' Angie took a deep breath and began.

'"Dear Angie" – don't know why he bothered putting

"Dear" – "I know you will be upset, but I feel the time has come for us to part. It's not working for me any more, and I have been very lucky to find Lisa, a sweet girl, an opera singer like me. We've known each other for two years" – TWO YEARS the bastard's been seeing her – "and she is expecting my child. It's right for her to live with me here. Therefore" – "THEREFORE"! How pedantic is that? – "I must ask you to find somewhere else to live, Angie, and move out as soon as you reasonably can. I thank you for the happy years we've had. Yours, Graham.'"

'Hang on, Angie … no … don't trash your laptop.' Laura put a restraining hand on Angie.

'I'd like to smash it over his head,' Angie growled.

Vati was looking down at me from the top of the bookshelf. He was sending me a telepathic thought. 'Why are you rolling around purring in the middle of all that human rage?'

I sent a thought right back at him. 'Because I'm a support cat. It's my job.'

'Don't trash your stuff!' Laura said.

Angie's wild eyes alighted on one of Graham's shirts she had been ironing earlier. She got up and ripped it from the hanger. She tore into it like a cat tearing at a piece of meat, chucking the strips of it high into the air. I glanced at Vati. Should we play with those tantalising ribbons of frayed shirt? Vati didn't think so. But I was feeling rebellious. I got down, aware that my eyes had gone black with excitement. I picked up a long strip of shirt in my teeth and went into the kitchen. I wanted it on a slippery floor where I could twirl with it.

'He's taking it out in the snow!' said Laura, and suddenly the two women were laughing hysterically.

I mean ... I was only doing my job as a support cat ... and today it was turning tears into laughter.

When Laura had gone, I crept back onto Angie's lap, and the crying started again, quietly this time.

'Thank you, Timba,' she sobbed. 'Why is the Universe doing this to us?'

I looked up at Vati who was still on the bookshelf and suggested he came down to help me console Angie. He did come down, still with that strange, lemon-bright look in his eyes, but he didn't come to Angie. He sat with his back to us in the window, fascinated by the snow now magically falling in large flakes.

Angie stopped ranting and was ominously quiet. She stared at the floor and didn't look once at the snow. I trusted Angie. I was sure she would take me with her, wherever she went, and Vati too.

But Vati made his feelings perfectly clear. He came down from the windowsill, avoided Angie, and jumped into Graham's favourite chair. Deliberately he curled up on a blue sweater Graham had left there, and went to sleep.

I was shocked. Vati was making a statement. He was going to stay with Graham.

I loved my brother. I needed him.

Now it was my turn to feel betrayed.

Weeks passed, and Angie did nothing but sit in the window, stare out at the garden, and cry. She did talk to Laura when she came, bringing flowers and hugs. One day Laura showed her the snowdrops standing stiffly in the winter wind, crowds of them under our apple tree. 'I can't bear to look at them,' Angie said. 'Graham and I planted them together when I came here. I can't look at anything beautiful any more. Only Timba and Vati.'

When Leroy was there, she made an effort to be happy, giving him what was left of her joyful spirit. Leroy was not convinced. 'Why are you sad, Angie?' he asked, and brought her little gifts of cards he had made and pictures of lions he had drawn.

'That's brilliant!' she gasped when he handed her a detailed drawing of a lion, done in white on black paper. 'You've got the curly mane so well, and the paws . . . but . . . there's something powerful . . . it's his eyes! They're really alive.'

Leroy glowed. 'It's my best picture,' he said, 'but you can keep it. I'm doing an even better one.'

Angie proudly put the picture in a frame and hung it next to the poster of the White Lions above the fridge in the kitchen.

'Shouldn't you be taking things down, not putting them up?' asked Graham.

'Oh don't you worry ... I'm making plans.' Angie looked at him coldly.

'What plans are those?'

'That's for me to know, and you to find out.'

She picked me up and carried me outside into the crisp blue light. The noontide sun was pale and bright, and the twigs of the apple tree glistened with frost. A single apple still hung there, like a reminder of fruitful times. The snowdrops trembled a little as some creature disturbed them. 'A bee!' shouted Leroy. 'Look, Angie. It's massive. Why is it out in the winter? It's too cold for bees.' He sent a puff of breath steaming into the light.

'Oh she's got a fur coat,' said Angie.

'But where does she live? And how do you know it's a she?'

'It's probably a queen bumblebee,' Angie said, 'and she's got a cosy nest under some long grass.'

'She's brave,' said Leroy. 'Queen bees gotta be brave.' Not for the first time Leroy's words did something to Angie. She stood up straighter, and carried me to the gate from where we could see the distant landscape.

'See those dark blue hills, Timba?' she said. 'That's where we're going. Far away, over those hills and across a shining river. We shall find a little terraced cottage with a garden, my mum's old place.'

'Am I coming, Angie?' asked Leroy, his face anxious as he sidled close.

'Yes, you're coming.' Angie smiled. 'And Timba and Vati. But we've got to cross our fingers and hope I get a job.'

'Is your mum there now?' Leroy asked. 'She could be my nan.'

'Sadly no, Leroy. She would have loved to be your nan, but she died three years ago, and left me the cottage. It was let to a young couple, but now it's empty ... so we can go there. We might have to decorate it ... but you'll help me, won't you? It'll be fun.'

'Can I paint lions on the walls?'

'Yes, you can paint one lion on one wall. I'd love that.' Angie began to sparkle, like her old self.

'What about my mum?' said Leroy. 'She won't know where I am.'

'Yes she will. We'll write the address down for her ... and she can come and visit you.'

'IF she turns up.' Leroy looked sad. He kicked at the frosty grass with his small foot. 'My mum don't want me, do she, Angie?'

'She does, Leroy. She's just stressed and needs to be by herself for a while.'

Leroy shook his head. 'She don't want me. It's true.'

Angie gave him a cuddle. 'I care about you, Leroy. I'm here for you, no matter what. OK?'

'And Timba?'

'And Timba . . . yes, he loves you, don't you, Timba?'

I did a purr-meow, and Leroy reached up to stroke me. We stood in the cold air, looking at those distant hills. Angie had given me a picture of our journey. Blue hills and a shining river, far away from where I was born. I didn't want to go.

'Don't be scared, Timba,' said Angie, reading my mind. 'You and Vati shall travel safely in a beautiful padded basket in the back of my car.'

A few days later Angie opened her laptop, her aura brightening. She stiffened, then stared at the screen. She leapt to her feet and shouted, 'YES!' and danced around the room snapping her fingers. 'I got the job! Thank you, Universe!'

On the day of the move, I was so angry with Vati that I attacked him . . . for real.

'I'm staying with Graham,' he said firmly.

'You can't do that!' I argued. 'We're brothers. We need each other.'

'Then you should stay.' Vati gave me a kiss on the nose, but I didn't respond. I was too angry for kissing.

'But I'm your protector,' I said, 'and we made a pact . . . two black kittens against the world.'

'That was kitten stuff,' Vati said. 'We're cats now.'

'Angie rescued you so that we could be together.'

'We have been together. Now it's time to move on.'

'Graham won't look after you the way Angie does,' I warned, 'and Lisa doesn't like cats.'

'She likes me. She thinks I'm cute.'

'But she might do something terrible to you, Vati.' As I spoke those words, I had a disturbing vision of Vati lying on the vet's table, very sick. Then I saw him hunched miserably in the corner of the sofa, shocked and depressed, the way Angie had been. 'Please, please don't do this, Vati,' I begged.

'I'm staying with Graham,' he said stubbornly, his paws locked neatly together, the tip of his tail twitching.

I flew at him, my fury beyond words. We rolled on the floor, screeching and yowling. For the first time ever, our claws were out and we were hurting each other. I bit Vati's ear and he fled upstairs. I thundered after him and cornered him on the landing. We faced each other like two furious dragons, our tails lashing. Vati's pink mouth was open in a convincing snarl, but his frightened eyes were black with disbelief.

Vati was lithe and strong, but I had the weight, and the fury, to dominate him. We might have seriously injured one another if Leroy hadn't intervened.

'Timba and Vati are killing each other!' he shouted to Angie who was stacking books into boxes.

'Oh they're just playing.'

'No . . . it's for real. And Vati's got a tuft of Timba's fur in his mouth.'

Leroy grabbed Vati and dragged him backwards. Vati struggled wildly, his claws out, leaving Leroy with long red scratches on his arms and hands. He chased Vati downstairs and lay on the floor, glowering at him under the sofa and cursing. 'You are a horrible cat, hurting my Timba, and scratching me.'

'Never intervene between two fighting cats,' said Angie wisely as she once again patched Leroy's scratches and calmed him down.

Eat, I thought, and headed for the kitchen, meowing. Predictably Angie came and fed me. 'Are you OK, Timba?' she asked, running her fingers through my fur. 'You look a bit ruffled. You've got such thick fur, you won't miss a bit of it.'

Vati stayed under the sofa.

Soon it was time for us to go, and Angie put me in the luxurious travelling basket. There was plenty of room for two cats.

Graham stood in the window silently, with Vati in his arms.

I never even got to say goodbye to my beloved brother.

And Angie didn't say goodbye to Graham, but stepped into the car with her shoulders back, and a brave smile on her face.

The parting was painful.

Driving down the lane we passed the gate to the horse field, and Poppy was standing there whinnying and kicking the gate with her hoof. Angie stopped the car and got out. 'Stay there … I won't be a minute,' she said to Leroy, and bounded over to Poppy.

The horse changed her shrill whinny to a soft whicker of greeting. She lowered her head, her chestnut mane fluttering like a flame in the breeze, her eyes loving and anxious. Angie flung her arms around the horse's neck and clung there as if she'd never let go. I knew, from the way her shoulders were heaving, that she was crying.

'Goodbye … darling, darling Poppy,' she wept. 'Laura will look after you, and one day … one day we'll be together again. Thank you for all the rides.' She paused, trying to breathe the tears away, and her voice cracked into fragments. 'Angie … will always … always love you.'

She might have stayed there hugging Poppy, but a car came along the narrow lane, and stopped, unable to get by.

'Sorry, guys!' Angie climbed back into the car and drove on, leaving Poppy watching us go, her dark eyes sad.

The three of us, Leroy, Angie and me, set off on our journey. Over the dark blue hills and across the shining river. The brave half of a broken family.

Chapter Twelve

ACROSS THE SHINING RIVER

The Spirit Lion managed to talk to me while we were bombing along in Angie's car. I was meowing a lot, wanting to tell the world how sad I felt about parting with Vati, how I didn't want to be a lonely cat and have to make decisions on my own. How frightened I was, despite the lovely travelling basket. How badly I wanted to go home.

Leroy kept twisting round to talk to me. 'It's OK, Timba. We going to live in WALES,' he said, 'and there's mountains and steam trains.'

'Timba's not impressed,' said Angie. 'It might be best to tell him we'll have a cosy home with a fire, and a kitchen with dishes of tuna.'

'Cheer up, Timba. You can have a massive dish of Whiskas chicken,' Leroy said. 'And there might be a cat next door you can play with.'

I heard him, but couldn't stop meowing. It was like crying. The contact with Leroy did help marginally, his big eyes looking at me in concern, and his finger pushed through the top of the basket. A tiny speck of comfort in my hollow cave of grief and anxiety.

Angie had shown me the dark blue hills, but they didn't seem to be getting any closer. As for the shining river . . . I'd never seen a shining river, but I knew rivers had something to do with water. Bad news for a cat!

Exhausted from worrying, I quietened down and tried to go to sleep. When I closed my eyes, the voice of the Spirit Lion shook me. 'Stay awake, Timba,' he boomed. 'Pay attention to this journey, for one day you will need to find your way back. Watch the hilltops for stone towers and lone pine trees. Remember the shape of the hills.'

Even as he spoke, I remembered the hill with a stone tower that was visible from the top of the apple tree. We were driving close to it now. 'Glastonbury Tor,' said Angie.

'Who lives in that tower?' Leroy asked in a whisper. 'Does a giant live there?'

'No. No one lives there. It's an old church tower.'

'Does God live there?'

'Nobody knows,' said Angie.

'Remember the shape of the hills,' the Spirit Lion had said, so I stared, trying to imprint the hill with the stone tower on my memory. We drove on through the morning and the hills turned from blue to green as they loomed closer, and on top was a tall metal tower going up to the sky. I felt the earth energy changing. The air was colder, the land covered in scrubby brown heather, and sheep were grazing in bright green patches of grass. At the crest of the hill, I felt we had reached a point of no return, and I began to grieve for the home I had loved. For Vati. For Graham, and Poppy, and the warm rug by the wood burner.

It wasn't fair.

I wished I was brave like Angie. She drove on, bushy and alert like a squirrel, ready to change, take risks and leap into a new space. 'Home doesn't have to be a place,' she'd said. 'Home can be who you're with.' And she'd shared her courage with Leroy. For him it was an adventure.

'I'd climb up there. Right to the top,' said Leroy as we drove past the metal tower, 'and I wouldn't be scared. Then I could see all the way to Africa and see the White Lions!'

Angie smiled. 'Maybe you could.'

163

The precious poster of the White Lions of Timbavati was rolled up in the back of the car, on top of the bags and boxes of books, and Leroy's toys.

The Spirit Lion kept me busy noticing landmarks, but, tired from the stress, I did eventually nod off to sleep. The car droned on, and when I awoke the sun was higher in the sky, and the hills were a distant smudge of blue, behind us now. Leroy's cry of excitement woke me.

'Cor, that's MASSIVE!' he shouted. 'Look at that bridge. Is that a suspension bridge, is it? Is it, Angie?'

I sat up to see.

'Look, Timba! That's the shining river,' Leroy said. 'You could go fishing in there. Has it got tuna in there, Angie?'

I saw the shining river, awesome, like a heavy snake of water, and the long, long bridge stretching over it. Beyond were more hills, dark with trees.

'Don't talk to me for a minute ... I need to get this right,' said Angie, and her face looked stressed as we joined a noisy stream of traffic.

I braced myself, feeling the thunder of the lorries hemming us in as we hurtled towards the river. In the cold air the exhaust fumes were hot and poisonous. The howl of engines rang in my ears and my throat burned from meowing. Leroy turned his big eyes to look at me. 'It's

OK, Timba.' But I was crazed with fear. He touched me. 'Timba's fur is coming out!' he said, but Angie clutched the steering wheel and drove on looking even more like a hyped-up squirrel.

I meowed again; this time it was a loud wail of distress. My life was out of control. I was trapped. I was being taken into the blue beyond, without my permission.

Leroy was squealing with excitement and bouncing around in his seat. 'Can we stop ... please, Angie? I want to look at the river. I want to climb up the bridge ... I could go high up ... oh please stop.'

'I can't stop. It's the motorway.'

'Please, Angie. You never do anything I want. It's not fair.' Leroy kicked his feet on the floor of the car.

Angie spoke to him sharply. 'Sit still, or you'll make me lose control of the car. Just, for God's sake, don't have a tantrum right now, Leroy. Save it for later!'

I saw the gleam of a tear on Leroy's cheek, but he managed to keep quiet. Angie hardly ever shouted at him, and when she did he took notice.

We sped on across the bridge. It was like a highway in the sky with the energy and power of the river surging far below. 'Remember the bridge,' the Spirit Lion said. How could I forget!

Where was Vati now? How far away? If only Angie would stop and open the travelling basket. I'd jump out and head back home on burning paws, my tail kinked over my back. But what chance would a little cat have on that hectic road?

My meows grew ever louder and more echoing. I was haunted by the thought that Vati, the wise one, had made the right decision ... to stay at home ... while I had made the wrong one.

'You must learn to trust,' said the Spirit Lion. 'Trust Angie. She's your earth-angel.'

By now we were driving on calmer roads through a dark forest. I paid attention to that. Even from the car, I could smell the trees and the creatures who lived there.

'We're nearly there,' Angie kept saying, and we emerged from the forest and headed downhill towards a town in a green valley. Angie drove on, but I wanted her to stop. I sensed danger. It came to me in a smell ... of something that didn't belong in this quiet green land. It got stronger and stronger.

'Timba's really scared, Angie,' said Leroy. 'He's got his tail bushed out.'

Why didn't Angie stop? Why was she driving on, into that unknown danger? It wasn't the smell ... it was a feeling. A sense of anger and displacement. It wasn't human! It was animal. More animal than I'd ever believed existed in our quiet green countryside.

'A zoo!' Leroy shouted, and Angie did slow down. She wasn't frightened like me, but she obviously didn't like seeing the zoo.

'Can we go in?' Leroy asked, and then answered his own question with a big sigh. 'I get it. Not now! But can we, one day?'

Angie drove slowly past some high walls with wire along the top, and two tall iron gates.

'I didn't know this was still here,' she said. 'I can't believe they haven't closed it down. It's a private zoo, and those animals are not happy in there. I can feel their desperation. Let's get clear of it.' She drove on very fast, and I relaxed a bit as the smell faded away. I hoped we weren't going to live near that zoo.

'You haven't let me do anything I wanted.' Leroy pouted and started to cry. 'I wanted to climb up the bridge, and I wanted to see if there were fish in the river. Then I wanted to see if there were bears in that forest . . . and you wouldn't let me.' He kicked angrily at the car floor.

Angie was kind. 'Aww, don't cry,' she said. 'Poor Leroy . . . I know it's tough, and you've been SO good. We'll do all those things when we're settled in. I'll need your help with Timba. He's terribly frightened, poor love, and you're so good with him now.'

Leroy calmed down. He turned to look at me. 'I'm

good now, Timba,' he said. 'Don't be scared. I'll look after you.'

Despite my plans to run away, I tried to settle down in the new house. Angie put my basket next to the Aga in the kitchen so I was cosy. It wasn't quiet like Graham's house. We could hear voices and traffic, and the rumble of huge shining aeroplanes which made the cups rattle. At first Leroy watched them constantly and asked Angie where they were going and why.

'Do they go to Africa?'

Angie shrugged. 'Maybe ... yes, I think there is a flight to Johannesburg.'

'Is that near Timbavati?'

'I don't know, Leroy. We'll look on the internet later.'

She dismissed it as unimportant, but I could see the dreams streaming through Leroy's mind. Dreams too big and intense to share.

The first time I was let out into the small square of garden, I remembered what Vati had taught me, and checked it out, walking slowly over the grass, feeling energies through my sensitive paws. I found a place where moles were living under the ground, I found an underground spring, and I found an energy line. It was in an odd place, close to a big stone in the wall of the house. Talking to Vati seemed possible when I sat there, but the contact was muffled. I missed him so much.

I kept an eye on Angie, who was getting used to a new job, and making new friends. She came home tired, and Leroy was difficult and demanding. He wanted every last bit of Angie's love and energy.

Leroy was obsessed with the zoo, and he pestered Angie every day. 'Why can't we go? I've never been to a zoo.'

'I will not spend my money visiting THAT PLACE,' Angie declared. 'When we have time I'll take you to a proper zoo where they care about the world's wildlife.'

'But I want to go to that one,' Leroy argued. I saw the look in his eyes. He was going to go there, no matter what, with or without Angie. I sensed it burning in his soul.

In the spring Angie bought Leroy a bike and a helmet to wear. Straight away, Leroy disappeared. He whispered goodbye to me and his eyes flashed with excitement. 'I've got a bike, Timba. Now I can go to the zoo.' I sat on the windowsill and watched him wheel the bike into the road.

'Don't go too far, Leroy. Just up and down outside, and be careful,' Angie called from the kitchen.

'Yeah ... OK. See you later,' Leroy shouted. He disappeared down the road at full throttle, pedalling with such energy that I thought the bike would fall apart. He was pushing it and pulling it at the same time, and lifting the front wheel off the floor, then banging it down.

I sat on the doorstep, and waited for him to come back.

Soon Angie was standing in the street looking for him, her eyes anxious. 'Where has he gone?'

I knew, but how could I tell Angie? I followed her up and down the street with my tail up, wanting to help, and in the end she picked me up. I tried sending her images, but she didn't get them. All I could do was cuddle against her and purr as she got more and more anxious, and cross with herself. 'How could I have been so stupid? Oh God, if he gets hurt on that main road, I'll never forgive myself.'

The next-door neighbour, Issy, got involved, and her cat came out too, and sat glaring at me. He was a portly tabby with one ear folded down, and he hadn't made friends with me, even though we'd been through each other's cat flaps.

'Leroy's such a wild impulsive child,' Angie told Issy.

'You can't take yer eyes off the little buggers these days,' Issy said. 'Especially boys. I'm glad my lot are grown-up. They all had bikes, and skateboards, and I spent half my life in A&E with 'em. But sometimes you just have to let 'em go and let 'em learn, that's what I say.'

'You're right,' Angie said, but her eyes still searched up and down the road. 'But Leroy had such a bad start. I have to protect him from himself.'

'Let's put the kettle on,' said Issy kindly. 'And by the time we've had a coffee, he'll be back, Angie, you'll see.'

Angie looked tempted, but she shook her head. 'Thanks, Issy, it's kind of you, but I can't. I must find him. I'd better get the car out.' She put me down on the garden wall. 'Will you keep an eye out for him, Issy? I'll drive to the park and other places he might go. He can't have gone far.'

I did a purr-meow. Leroy was already far away, I knew that, and I so wanted to tell Angie. I had to watch her drive off in totally the wrong direction. I went to sit on the energy point by the big stone, and called the Spirit Lion by sending a silent message into the light. He came instantly, filling the garden with radiance. I asked him why humans were so limited in their ability to communicate.

'Centuries ago they took the life out of language,' he said, 'by carving it into stone. Now they scribble it with pens, and tap it out on keyboards. All they want is to see it, to read it, and to them that is truth. In doing so they condemned telepathy and called it witchcraft.'

'Witchcraft?' I asked, and felt my spine turn to ice. Had I once been a witch's cat? The memory sailed into my mind. A proud memory. I had been a witch's cat, and the witch had been Angie! We had talked wordlessly to each other. We had healed animals and plants, and we had tele-ported along the golden roads. It was my best lifetime.

The Spirit Lion saw my thoughts. 'Humans can still do it,' he said. 'They have only to remember . . . and some of them do. That's why cats are so important. Cats are fascinating to humans. Cats are wordless communicators, and teachers.'

'So how can I teach Angie? How can I reach her now?'

'When she wants to learn, she will sit with you,' said the Spirit Lion. 'In the meantime you can only be there for her, let her make her mistakes and just love her. Some of her mistakes, like going in the wrong direction, are meant to happen. It is part of the plan. She can't control Leroy. What he is doing right now is part of his destiny.'

'What is he doing?' I asked, and the Spirit Lion fell silent. His eyes met my questioning stare. 'Merge with me,' he said, 'and I'll show you.' I became one with him as my aura blended with his radiance where he shared his thoughts wordlessly.

First he showed me Leroy's bike. It was lying in the dappled sunlight under an oak tree, and Leroy's red helmet shone in the piles of leaf mould and mossy roots. Leroy was nowhere to be seen. But my hackles were up, my whiskers twitching. That smell! A stench of confined animals . . . their droppings, their hot fur, the tang of fear, and the smoulder of desperation.

Once the smells settled into our consciousness, there were sounds to identify. Unfamiliar, strident bird cries and the flutter of wings, the clank of rusty metal, the high-pitched chattering of active, hyped-up creatures I couldn't identify. We listened, and heard the wind teasing petals from blossom and sweeping it into corners. Then the scrape-scrape of a lion's paws on rough concrete, an endless rhythm, a hopelessness as he padded to and fro, never going anywhere except from one wall to the other.

And then we saw Leroy.

He was clinging to the outside of the boundary wall, his feet wedged into the cracks between bricks, his eager eyes searching upwards for a way through the strands of wire along the top. I felt moved. Leroy was brave. Braver than me, and I was a cat!

Safe in the haven of my Spirit Lion, I watched, and hoped, and tried to send Leroy love. Painfully he climbed on, helped by a sturdy ivy plant, dragging himself up and up until he was looking down at the padding lion with an awestruck smile. The lion glanced up at him, sniffed, and continued padding as if he didn't care. He'd been there, done that, and didn't want to be bothered with humans.

Leroy's hands stretched towards the wire. He touched it, and all hell broke loose. A deafening siren started, sending the animals into panic, and a man burst out of a door, a shovel in his hand. His angry eyes scanned the top of the wall, and saw Leroy clinging there.

'What the HELL are you doing?' he bellowed. 'Get

down off that wall right now or I'll come out and drag you down.'

Shaking with fright, Leroy scrambled backwards. We heard the tearing of the ivy plant as he fell in an explosion of leaves. Then he ran, rubbing the blood from his arms, seized his bike and flung himself onto it. Leaving the red helmet lying in the leaf mould, he pedalled wildly into the traffic and headed home.

At that point the Spirit Lion gently disengaged from me. We both knew I had to be a support cat for when Leroy made it home.

When he finally came riding up the street, Angie was pacing up and down like the lion.

'Where have you BEEN?' she asked.

Leroy shrugged.

'Nowhere,' he said.

I ran to him with my tail up, and, while Angie ranted, I purred and loved and showed her how to welcome a tired, distraught child.

I got used to the place, but the homesickness never left me. I was OK when Angie and Leroy were there, but when Angie was at work, and Leroy at school, I was left alone for long hours. I missed Vati terribly, and I missed Graham. I missed Poppy, and the chickens, and the freedom of a big garden. Here the back garden was boxed in by other gardens where there were cats who didn't want to be friends. I tried to establish a territory, but it was limited. The spring was cold and rainy, so I spent hours indoors by the Aga, or sitting in the window. Angie and Leroy played with me and brushed me, and then I was a happy cat. But I yearned for those exciting playtimes with Vati.

In my heart I didn't feel at home.

Angie sat with me on her lap when Leroy was in bed. She shared her sadness with me. She missed Graham. She hated Lisa. She felt betrayed. 'But we must make the best of it, Timba,' she often said. 'Think positive.' Then she would talk about Leroy. 'I love that boy. I so want to help him. He's got such a talent . . . and such dreams. We have to help him make those dreams come true, Timba. Don't we?' I always agreed with a yes–meow and lots of purring.

One wet Sunday the sparks were flying from both their auras as Angie and Leroy sat in front of Leroy's laptop. Curious, I jumped onto the table and sat with them, looking at the screen. They were looking at the White Lions!

'Don't walk on the keyboard, Timba.' Leroy moved me gently aside, but I wanted to touch noses with one of those lions. I stared and stared, feeling my neck getting longer. Slowly I stretched forward, my whiskers tingling with excitement, and touched noses, nicely. The lion didn't respond, and Angie and Leroy laughed at me, but I felt I'd reached across the world and given wordless love to this brave, important lion.

'It says their coats can be whiter than the whitest snow,' said Angie. 'A White Lion is the most sacred animal in Africa.'

'Yeah, but they're not albinos,' Leroy said. 'No one knows where the White Lions came from. It's a mystery! Come on, Angie, let's read the legends again.' He clicked something and a load of writing appeared instead of the interesting pictures of lions. 'I can nearly read this now . . . but you help me with the long words, Angie.'

'WOW! Listen to this,' said Angie. '"The name Timbavati is from an ancient Shangaan language –" AND – "it means *the place where star lions come down from the heavens*". WOW.'

Leroy's face shone. He searched the block of text on the screen and pounced on another word. '"Golden",' he said. '"Timbavati is on a golden . . ." I can't read that, Angie.'

My spine began to tingle. A golden road, I thought.

Angie took over the reading. '"Timbavati is on the Golden Nile Meridian,"' she read.

'What's that?'

'It's an energy line . . . a sacred pathway across the

world,' Angie whispered, and her words excited me so much that I did an amplified extended-meow. More laughter. I didn't think it was funny. Miffed, I stared into Angie's eyes. 'Timba understands that, don't you, lovely cat?' she said warmly, and got a yes-meow in return.

Leroy was racing ahead, his eyes searching the writing. '"Sphinx,"' he said. 'It's on the same line. What's a sphinx?'

'Google it,' said Angie, and Leroy tapped the keyboard and clicked. The screen flickered, and a picture appeared of the ancient stone sphinx in the desert. It spooked me, and my memory flipped into life. I remembered a time, centuries ago, when Vati and I had been proud Egyptian cats. We had played in the hot sun, and slept between the glistening stone paws of that mighty sphinx.

'Timba understands this too.' Leroy looked into my eyes, and in that moment I understood something else. Leroy was developing telepathy. He could read my thoughts. 'Do you miss Vati, Timba?'

I walked over the forbidden keyboard and kissed Leroy on the nose.

Chapter Thirteen

JOURNALESQUE

Chapter Thirteen

JOURNEY SOUTH

It happened very quickly.

One minute I was a contented cat, and the next I was faced with a life-changing challenge.

'You're the best cat in the world, Timba.' Angie pressed her cheek against my fur, and I looked up at her, blinking my eyes slowly and purring. 'I hope we never lose you.'

Odd that she said those words, as if she sensed I was on the brink of a momentous decision. I took my job as a support cat very seriously. Most cats only had one human to look after. I had two. Angie, who was still hurting from Graham dumping her, still missing Poppy, and trying too hard to be an earth-angel to Leroy. And Leroy, who needed me even more.

On that drowsy afternoon in late summer, my life should have been blessed. I should have been full of gratitude for a home where I was loved and pampered. I was the best cat in the street and, when I sat up on the garden wall, everyone who passed by admired me. 'Aren't you beautiful!' and 'What a magnificent cat,' and 'You're so fluffy, and so friendly. I wish you were my cat.' I soaked it all up, like fan mail. It was like an insurance too. I knew that if I followed any one of those adoring fans down the road, they would adopt me.

But something was missing from my life: Vati. I tried to get used to it, the way Angie was coping without Graham. The way she still laughed and smiled and got on with it. I was managing OK, until the momentous decision arrived like an unstoppable rain cloud darkening the sunlight.

I was sitting against the wall, close to the big stone in the place where I'd sensed a precious line of communication. My direct chat line to Vati. So far our long-distance chats had been misty but joyful. Vati had appeared with his tail up, looking sleek and mystic. He told me he was OK with Graham and Lisa. He told me Lisa had a baby girl, Heidi, and Heidi was crawling all over the house like a cat.

The Spirit Lion had taught me how to sense the energy line with my pads, so I did that now, and visualised Vati's winsome little face with the white dot on the nose. His eyes flashed up before me, black and terrified. My paws began to burn with pain. 'What is it? What's happened?' I asked, but Vati seemed totally unable to communicate. I tried and tried and got no response. Darkness inked its way along the golden pathway, right into my heart.

I sat there, stunned.

Something terrible had happened to Vati.

I ran to Angie. She was leaning on the garden wall, watching the road. 'Leroy should be back soon, from his first day at big school,' she told me, and scooped me into her arms. Normally I would have purred and made a fuss of her, but now I felt my heart was breaking.

I had to go.

I had to find Vati.

Sadly and silently, I licked Angie's dear face which was warm from the sun. It was my last chance to love her. I should say goodbye nicely, I thought. I should purr. But I couldn't. I felt like a cat torn in two.

The best I could manage was a long stare into her sensitive eyes, and immediately Angie saw that something was wrong. 'What's the matter, Timba?'

I couldn't bear to say goodbye. I slid out of her arms and jumped down to the pavement.

'Timba? Are you OK? Timba . . .'

I half turned, flicked my tail, and gave Angie a silent meow. Then I trotted purposefully down the road, my tail down, my heart heavy. I didn't look back, even when I heard the school bus, and the sound of Leroy dragging his school bag along the ground. He'd had a bad day. And I was a support cat. What was I doing?

The only glad thought in my mind was that I'd eaten all of my lunch, every last crumb of the delicious, easy food Angie made for me. I was healthy and strong, my coat luxurious and well brushed. It would keep me warm through the lonely nights of my journey south ... back through the dark forest, and over the shining river, to the green hills where I'd been born.

Angie thought I would come back, like I always did. She'd trusted me, and let me be free, and it had been the best life a cat could have. She'd patiently helped Leroy, taught him how to love me the way a cat should be loved, and he was getting it right. I had grown to love Leroy. Now he'd think I'd abandoned him.

For a long time I heard Angie and Leroy calling me, but I trotted on automatically, as if my mind and body were totally separate. On and on through the streets, not even pausing to put my tail up and let somebody stroke me, not worrying about traffic or dogs, or which way to go. I knew. My instinct was crystal clear, and I let it guide me south. I kept going, until the voices and memories faded, and a sense of detachment hung over me like the shadow of night.

Crossing the road was VERY scary. I spent a lot of time crouched under parked cars, watching for a clear space. Judging the speed of cars was a skill I hadn't developed and, after a couple of near misses, my confidence was shaken. The endless, confusing streets and the exhaust fumes gave me a headache. In the deepening yellow light of late afternoon, I took refuge in a garden. The gate was open, so I crept in and hid under an evergreen covered in scarlet berries. I scent-marked its stout trunk and leaned against it, feeling the calm energy of the plant world stabilising my agitated heartbeat. It was good to have a wall between me and the traffic.

I listened, hoping to detect the last calls from Angie and Leroy, but now I was too far away, lost in the roar of a town I had never bothered to explore. I'd been a home cat, my territory modestly limited to the surrounding gardens. The listening seeded an ache in my heart, a yearning to hear the voices one last time: 'Timba. TIM ... BA.' Who would call me Timba now?

No one would know who I was. I'd chosen to leave my home; now it became clear I was leaving behind my identity. I was any old cat now. Nameless and shameless. If I was going to live without love, then I'd have to be tough.

The hunter instinct surfaced alongside the hunger now growling around my belly. I surveyed the strange garden and the imperious blackbirds hopping about on the lawn. My tail twitched. Catching one would be easy. But less convenient than the tasty supper Leroy would have been giving me right now.

But, hey, this house had a cat flap! I was powerful and bossy. I could deal with any cat who might be in there. Go for it, I thought. Stealthily I prowled up the path, low to the ground, and glided through the cat flap. Inside was an array of dishes on the floor, and one had a substantial dollop of fishy-smelling cat food. Nobody was there so I scoffed it down.

'You cheeky cat! OUT!' came the voice, and a woman who looked like a toad came at me with a squeegee mop. No one had ever treated me like this! I half put my tail up and tried to cat smile at her, but my friendliness seemed to enrage her even more. 'That's my cat's food!' she shrieked. 'OUT ... go on ... OUT!'

I'd never been afraid of a human, and I wasn't now. A few minutes of tail up and rubbing lovingly round her legs would soon melt her cold heart. But it didn't work out.

With a scrabble of paws, a beefy little dog charged into the kitchen, almost airborne in its rush to get to me.

I looked at it disdainfully, and wished I knew how to laugh. The entire dog was vibrating with its hysterical barking, even its ridiculously short legs and flippy little ears.

You don't turn your back on dogs. Your back end is vulnerable, especially the tail. My mum Jessica had perfected the art of reversing through a cat flap, but I hadn't tried it, and hadn't needed to until now.

I arched my back and made a savage snarly face. Predictably, the dog ran out of steam and stopped a few feet away from me, its white body trembling, its eyes uncertain. Majestically I crab-walked towards the cat flap, my tail lashing. I whipped round and dived out through it, and felt a horrible tearing sensation as the dog ripped a tuft of hair from my tail. What a cheek!

I fled down the garden and straight across the road into the path of an oncoming white van. There was a screech of tyres, and a volley of swearing. I changed my mind in mid-air, my whiskers brushing the hot rubber wheel as I turned and dashed back. Thoroughly frightened, I crept, black-eyed, under the same evergreen and stayed there. The tip of my tail was sore and bleeding, and it looked awful. Tails are sensitive and important, and that feisty little dog had ruined mine. I attended to it immediately, licking and cleaning and rearranging the fur that was left.

My nerves were shattered and I remembered what Angie had said when Leroy had squeezed me. 'His little bones are like matchsticks.' An unexpected flood of respect for my body came to me now. I needed to rest. Yet something pushed me onward. I wouldn't stop until I found the edge of the noisy town.

Many streets later I finally reached the quiet. Stubble fields stretched away from me, the edges cushioned with tussocks of wild flowers and grasses. My tired paws sank into the softness and found it still warm from the sun. So welcome, now that the twilight had a taste of cold, as if winter might arrive in the night.

I made myself a round nest under an ash tree. Vati had taught me about different trees and their effect on cats. Ash trees were stabilising and healing. This one splayed its leaves over me like a guardian of the plant world. I slept under it for hours, and when I awoke, my fur felt damp.

Against the night sky the fields and hedges were the colour of blackberries. Above me the stars seemed to be entangled in the ash tree's branches.

At midnight at home I would usually walk around on Leroy's bed, loving him while he slept. Or I'd go downstairs and find Angie still awake at the table, her head bent over a pile of children's school books, a red pen in her hand. Or she'd be in the kitchen baking midnight cakes. We'd have a cuddle and, if the night was clear, she'd carry me outside to look at the stars. Those same stars I was looking at now.

The thought made me unbearably homesick. What had I done? How had my love for Vati taken precedence over everything I treasured? I vowed that, when I found him, I would bring him home, home where he belonged with me and Angie and Leroy.

I climbed into the ash tree, glad that my eyes were so good at night. Up there everything was crystal sharp, the leaves black, the stubble fields a shimmering silver; the distant rim of the sky glowed orange, and lights twinkled from the town I had left. I turned my face to the south, and on that horizon loomed the forest, my next destination. A beam of excitement cut through the heavy mist of homesickness. The forest was one part of my journey which appealed to the wild cat still curled up in my soul.

The Spirit Lion turned up at dawn. In my nest of dry grass, I was listening to the chatter of gathering swallows, flocks of them swooping and diving over the fields, moving south without appearing to do so.

The Lion came slinking across the networks of gossamer that bedecked the stubble and festooned the brambles around the ash tree. He came from the east, silent, almost invisible, but real. He took a long time to arrive, as if demonstrating his manifestation skills.

I waited, feeling better just knowing he was there for me: he was choosing to find me. Was he going to send me back home to Angie? Would he tell me what was wrong with Vati?

Slow and thoughtful, he enfolded me in those giant paws, the mane tumbling like a waterfall, the eyes guarding a secret more global than the concerns of a fluffy black cat.

He began with wordless communication, loving me, encouraging me to relax and purr. The purring reassured me, and for once I was purring for ME. Purring was not only for humans: it was for me to calm myself, to heal my hurts. To send a message across the Earth.

The Spirit Lion looked satisfied when I understood this startling truth. It came close to what Vati had tried to teach me about the energy lines.

'Planet Earth is full of messages,' the Spirit Lion said. 'You must learn a different way of listening, Timba, a listening that is more like touching. Stretch out on the earth and listen with the whole of your being. Do this often on your journey, for if you don't you will become lost.'

'Vati needs me urgently,' I said. 'I can't go fast enough to reach him. It's a long way.'

The Spirit Lion was silent, his eyes absorbing my words. Then he said, 'Winter is coming, Timba. You must go quickly. Don't run with your feet, think with them, and be smart. Your times of stillness must be used for attunement and meditation.'

'Meditation?' I asked, curious. Angie had used that

word passionately and often, but it had drifted over me in my preoccupation with food and play.

'Meditation,' the Lion repeated, 'is like daydreaming, Timba. When the body is still, the mind can travel through space and time. Gaze back across the centuries and reclaim the wisdom and intelligence of the cat. Much of it has been used to heal and support humans, but you can use it on your journey to manipulate humans into giving you the right kind of help.'

'Vati can do that kind of stuff,' I said.

'Vati is a highly evolved, supersensitive being,' said the Spirit Lion. 'That's why you are perfect together . . . twin souls. Between you, you have all the gifts.'

'We're brothers,' I said proudly. 'The sons of Solomon.'

'Yes . . . but for now, Timba, you must do the work of two cats. Vati cannot work right now. Your strength and pragmatism, and Vati's sensitivity. You are right, he needs you urgently . . . urgently.' The Spirit Lion became ominously quiet. His presence turned misty, and the light around him flickered alarmingly.

'Don't go,' I said. Our conversation wasn't finished, and he was drifting precariously. 'You haven't told me what's wrong with Vati.'

The Spirit Lion darkened. The colours of night filtered down through his curly mane. A frown gathered like a thunderstorm on his brow.

'Don't go,' I repeated, suddenly gripped by a fear beyond anything I had ever experienced. This wasn't fear of getting hurt or lost. This was cosmic. Cosmic fear of some undiscovered mistake that was building into a global catastrophe.

The Spirit Lion's last words were a hollow whisper echoing in my soul. 'I can't say it,' he breathed, and the hush of cosmic sadness descended from the morning sky. The birds fell silent. The air was becalmed, and the beads of dew on the gossamer lost their sparkle. Leaves fell like tears from the ash tree.

The Spirit Lion breathed in deeply. 'I can't say it,' he said again. 'It is universal. A happening, a terrible happening that is seeding fear in cats . . . all over the Earth . . . all . . . over . . .' he whispered, and the sadness eclipsed his shining light. In seconds he was gone.

I sat there, numb and shocked, watching a bank of white mist stealing in from the valley, as if the energy of the Spirit Lion had been dissolved and was floating away, shape-shifting, becoming a cloud billowing over the bright sun.

My Spirit Lion had gone . . . not joyfully . . . but immersed in sadness. There was something out there he couldn't bear to talk about. He'd given me his love, and his wisdom. Now he'd left me. Once again, at my time of greatest need, I was alone.

The mist settled like a fleece over the fields, hiding the landscape from me when I needed to see it. I wanted to work out which way to go. I tried to talk to Vati, to tell him I was on my way to rescue him, but all I saw was the black of his eyes, and the stillness of his crouched body. For some reason Vati was not moving, and not communicating. Alive, but closed down. Unresponsive, unmotivated, numb.

What had happened to this beautiful, creative little cat?

I knew in my bones that, if I didn't get to him soon, Vati would will himself to die.

Chapter Fourteen

THE DARK FOREST

The Spirit Lion told me not to run without thinking first, but I pushed on relentlessly, driven by the pain in Vati's eyes and the urgency of his need. I didn't think of the distance that separated us, but focused on one day at a time. I ran along the hedges, parallel to the road. Flocks of birds flew ahead of me, feeding on scarlet berries that bobbed in the branches above. I felt like an impostor. The magpies and crows cursed me in their raucous voices, and the blackbirds warned each other about me. No one wanted a fluffy black cat in the countryside. For a cat who was used to lots of love and attention, it felt bleak and lonely.

Late afternoon was the time when foxes emerged from their holes, hungry, full of energy. I was wary of them, but quickly found I could outstare an interested fox, or out-smart it by climbing a tree. But after several encounters, my wariness mushroomed into fear. A fox could kill me if it caught me off guard, or sleeping.

As I drew near to the forest, another creature scared me: a buzzard that flew out of the trees with wings like giant hands. Its cry haunted me because it resembled a cat meowing, and it swooped low and flexed its powerful wings above me so that I felt the rush of air from its feath-ers, and saw the talons and the cruel yellow eyes. And there were always two buzzards, hunting together, watch-ing for movement in the grass.

Tension began to build in my mind, tiring me, not allowing me the rest I needed.

Towards evening the mist cleared and the sun hung low and bright, like a peach on fire. On the opposite side of the sky the moon was rising, and it was pink. I hurried on, up a hill, heading south between sun and moon. Aching tiredness slowed me down to a steady trot, my eyes fixed on the luminous sky at the crest of the hill. Would the hill never end?

Twilight was falling as I reached the top, and the cool colours of night stained the brim of the sky. Exhausted, I lay down under a pine tree, glad of its soft carpet of nee-dles and moss. A perfect bed for a cat who needed to watch the stars and study the distant landscape.

All I needed was a plate of mashed chicken with gravy. Even if there had been a handy mouse, I was too tired to catch one. I slept and slept, my paws twitching as I crossed roads in my nightmare. Hunger gnawed at my dreams, and my tummy felt weak and empty. Nothing else disturbed me, and as usual I awoke at midnight. The moon was far away in the southern sky. Silent and pale, an owl passed by on muffled wings. It turned a heart-shaped face and checked me out with intelligent eyes. I looked back, proudly, unafraid of this creature of the night who had once terrorised me.

The owl turned in a wide arc and returned to check me out again. I thought of Vati and the way he had a mysterious rapport with wild creatures. How he'd searched their minds, and seen the good in them, the hunger, and the fun.

As the owl swooped by for a third time, I sent him a telepathic message. 'I'm Timba, and I'm on a long journey to find my brother Vati . . . because I love him.' I saw the message arrive like a spark of understanding in the owl's black eyes. I watched him hover over a tangle of grasses, and heard the swoosh of wing feathers when he pounced on some creature who had dared to pop out of a hole.

The next minute the owl dived towards me, looking at me with intense eyes. It hovered above me, pale wings catching a glaze of moonlight.

There was a soft thud, and a dead mouse, ready to eat, was dropped right in front of my paws. A midnight feast, delivered with style to a starving cat!

I looked up and meowed in astonishment, and the owl gave me a permissive sort of nod, screeched, and flew away.

Between me and the forest was a vast meadow in which a herd of cattle grazed. So far I'd been running along the hedgerows, day after day, crossing the occasional lane. Once I paused by an isolated cottage to see if it had a cat flap. The door was open and I slunk over the polished stone doorstep and peeped in at a table with food on it . . . and nobody there! Angie hadn't allowed me on the kitchen table, but I'd never been this hungry since I was a kitten. Moving smoothly like a cloud, I glided in, grabbed a cheese sandwich and fled back to the safety of the hedge. The butter and cheese tasted good but not the bread. Bread was bad for me, even with Marmite on it.

Tempted to hang around and become an accomplished thief, I found a sunny corner and tried to wash. I had brushed against a burdock plant and my lovely fur was matted with prickly burrs. Annoyed, I worked at getting them out and was distressed to find I couldn't shift them. I rolled on the floor, scratched, and tugged at my matted fur, but the burrs refused to come out and began to be painful. Angie had never let my fur get in such a state.

Time was passing. The leaves were falling, the song-birds silent, the nights longer. Winter was coming, and I would be cold and alone. The immediate challenge was the field of cattle. They weren't amiable milking cows. They were hefty young bullocks, alert and interested in anything that moved. The field was enormous, and I wasn't used to long runs. Short bursts of speed were OK. A field that huge, with no cover, looked impossible. The bullocks might surround me, and blow their hot breath at me, and toss me in the air, or even trample on me.

So I sat outside the gate in the middle of a lemon-scented patch of wild camomile, and once the bullocks had seen me and done some snorting and stamping, they got bored and wandered away. My only chance was to wait until they reached the far side of the field, then make a dash for it.

I had to believe that I could run that far, that fast, on tired paws at the end of the day! I waited ages for the cattle to retreat, and I was getting more and more agitated.

When the last bullock reached the far side, I made a run for it. Low and fast was how I wanted to go, but the turf was covered in thistles and cowpats, so I was jumping and dodging.

I was out in the open when I heard their roar and felt the thunder of their hooves. I ran for my life, my paws splashing through mud. The bullocks crossed the field in seconds, their tails in the air. I was going to die, horribly, in the pungent stench of them and the mud. I tried and tried to run faster, but there was no place to hide. Bewildered, I turned and found myself surrounded by steaming red-brown faces.

In my moment of need, Vati flashed into my mind, and I remembered the way he used his winsome little face and kinky tail to bewitch any creature who threatened him. The power of the cat! Come on, Timba, use it!

I sat down in the middle of those red-brown faces, and scrutinised their minds. Actually they didn't WANT to kill me. They were just having fun. If they killed me, it would be by accident, not intention.

I was terrified, but in control. The intense power of my absolute stillness shone like a dazzling star. Stiff whiskers gleaming, my aura fierce with light, I focused on one particular bullock. Eyeball to eyeball, we exchanged an animal rights agreement.

I, Timba, have a right to occupy my bit of Mother Earth, even if it's smaller than your bit. I, Timba, am a cat, and cats have been here longer than cattle. You are going to end up on someone's plate, covered in gravy and next to a potato. Whereas I, Timba, will become an indispensable, pampered cat with supreme influence over my humans. Therefore, you will grant me free exit from this field, at my own pace, with my tail up.

Then I did something VERY brave. I walked towards the ring-leader and kissed his outstretched nose. I visualised myself as a shining cat, my light so vivid that no one would harm me.

With deliberate slowness and calm, and with a flagrant wave of my tail, I walked away and on towards the forest. The bullocks trailed behind me, clumped together and at a respectful distance. Keep it slow, Timba, keep it slow, I was thinking, and finally... finally, I was out of the field. I even turned and blinked my golden eyes, a cheeky goodbye to the bemused red-brown faces.

After that, I had no more trouble from cattle, ever again.

It's important to have fun, even if you're miserable, I thought as I strolled into the towering twilight of the forest. My paws were sore, my once lovely fur matted with burrs, my heart heavy with the weight of Vati's mysterious problem. Added to that, if I sat thinking for too long I got homesick and wanted to turn back. But I was a young cat, bright-spirited and strong, and there was power in being totally alone in a place of magic.

Magic was everywhere in this forest. I sensed it shimmering between the leaves, teasing me with dancing patterns of light. Crisp autumn leaves floated down, twirling through the stillness, and landed light as cheese puffs. The urge to play with them tugged at the edges of my misery until I gave in and went totally mad, diving and sliding into them, leaping high in the air, my paws akimbo, my tail flying.

I felt brilliant. I was Timba again. My play got more and more creative. I hid behind the stout oak trunks, and leaped out, wild-eyed, my back and tail arched as I sped across the glade. Charged by the magic, I ran into another dimension. The joy was re-creating me: I was a spirit cat being born again from the tatty remains of a tired black cat with burrs in his fur.

I felt that Vati was there with me and my playing was drawing him out to the bright margins of his darkness.

Liberated, I whirled and capered until I heard laughter. At home I loved to generate laughter. Nothing made me happier. So, who was laughing at me, here in this lonely forest?

I paused, and found myself doing exactly what the Spirit Lion had told me to do: stretching out and touching the earth with the whole of my being. And listening.

My eyes had closed from sheer exhaustion, but I was in a state of trance. The laughter was high-pitched and silvery, and it was coming from hundreds of exquisite beings of light. Their eyes flickered as they laughed, not at me, but with me. These were beings of pure joy. Clustered high up in the trees, they too were listening to some finer, higher song from the Universe beyond.

I kept still and the tiny beings began to descend like glitter falling through the forest. They came closer and closer until I saw their colours, and felt their love cover me in a canopy of stars. And then I slept, like a dead cat sprawled across the forest floor, and I dreamed of a straight and secret path that would lead me to Vati. The path had the softest, most luminous green grass that healed my paws, and on either side of it rose tall plants with straight stems, growing densely and protectively together, like a guard of honour for me.

Day after day I trotted through the trees, sometimes running and leaping over clumps of plants, sometimes following narrow paths which looked promising as they wound between ferns. There were plenty of mice and voles for me to catch, as well as starlings, who descended in twittering flocks to feed on the berries, stripping whole trees bare in one sitting. They were easy prey as they paraded around the forest floor, driving their beaks into the ground to find worms and grubs. Mysteriously they moved as one mind, their plumage glistening with rainbows, their wings whirring as they took off in unison, darkening the sky with their swirling clouds.

The forest had hilltop places almost touching the sky, and I was drawn to them. Each time I expected to see the shining river, and the far-off land where Vati waited for me. I wanted to see the end of my journey. But each hill-top only gave me a view of another wooded hill, and another beyond. It was never-ending, and I started to feel downhearted. The nights were cold now and I chose to travel in the moonlight, sleeping in the daytime when the sun warmed my fur.

One night the moon seemed to be bobbing alongside me, silver white behind the black trees. The night was a dark crystal, sharp with frost, and all I heard was the whisper of my paws trotting through the cold. Ahead of me was a hill without trees, and the sky above it was coppery and alive with moving lights. At the top, I sat, spellbound, my tail twitching with excitement. Far away the river shone white in the moonlight, and the long bridge sparkled orange, like a necklace of beads strung across the water. There was the taste of traffic fumes in the frosty air, the hum of cars and lorries, their lights reflected in the water as they crossed the long bridge.

So far away . . . it both encouraged and frightened me. How could a little cat get safely across that busy bridge? I'd have to try.

On the forest floor the air was still but the west wind roared in the high branches as I spent many days sheltering miserably from a storm. I lost all sense of direction, and began to wonder if I was wasting precious time while Vati was edging closer and closer to death.

Utterly depressed, I curled up in the leaves, and tried to sleep, switch off, forget I was now a homeless, nameless cat on a mission. Rain glazed the surface of my fur, but I didn't bother to move. Starlings flew down, but I didn't bother to catch one.

Why bother? I was seriously lost.

My fur, which I'd been so proud of, was driving me mad. Itching, full of burrs, matted beyond belief, and, despite my efforts to groom myself, I ended up being sick from the hairballs I had somehow swallowed. There was even a piece of bramble caught in my tail.

So intense was my anxiety about Vati that when I finally saw the bridge again I didn't hesitate. I didn't stop and try to work out how best to cross it. I thought, Go for it, Timba, and soon I was trotting along the grassy edge of the slip road that led onto it.

I didn't expect it to make me ill, but it did, right from the start, down there in the haze of pollution that hung over the tarmac. The winter afternoon was dove grey and still. A yellowish white mist drifted over the river, mixing with the traffic fumes.

The slip road was easy, but once the grass disappeared there was nothing but iron and tarmac between me and the traffic. The lorries towered over me. The rush of air and the vibration threw me sideways. Each time it happened, I ended up crouching, pressing myself against the metal with my eyes closed. The noise was thunderous and relentless. It rang in my skull. The whoosh of each vehicle blasted gritty air through my fur, almost lifting me off the ground.

I glanced up a few times at the drivers, hell bent on crossing that bridge as fast as possible. Didn't anyone see me? Didn't anyone care about a fluffy black cat, all alone, trying to survive? Surely someone would stop and pick me up, wouldn't they? I was getting unbelievably tired. It needed every bit of my strength just to stay on the road and not be blown off balance, or knocked into the river far below.

Nobody stopped for me. I thought about the love I had given to humans. Was I invisible? Did I actually look like a cat now, or like a piece of rubbish blown into a corner? I had a go at putting my tail up and trying to look like a successful cat, but it was impossible. The next thundering lorry sent me rolling sideways until I hit the iron and scrabbled desperately to get back on my feet. And then a man shouted at me from a speeding car.

'Get off the bridge, you stupid cat! Go back. You'll be killed!'

The tone of his voice cut into my consciousness. I paused, realising I was not making progress. I was surviving, but only just, and for how long?

Turning to face the oncoming traffic, I saw the pathetic little distance I had covered, and realised how ill it had made me. My eyes stung so much it was hard to keep them open. My paws shook. My tail dragged in the oily dirt. Even breathing was painful.

In a moment of despair, I curled into a ball and pressed my face against the cool of the metal. What a place to die, I thought, here on this terrible bridge, alone, with no one to love me. I wanted to die on Angie's lap, or in her beautiful garden. Not here. Not like this.

That one thought made me decide to give up. I couldn't cross the bridge, but I could try to go back. Even to live again in the green forest with my matted fur and lonely heart had to be better than this. So, as long as I breathed, I would drag myself to a quiet haven where I could die in peace.

A blessed break in the traffic gave me a minute to recall a healing place. With absolute clarity I remembered the owl woman, Mrs Lanbrow, who had rescued me from the trolley. I saw her, and felt her, as if she was really with me, holding me in the glow of her hands. The memory encouraged me to try and save myself.

I didn't dare stand on my wobbly legs, for the rush of air from the rumbling lorries would have bowled me over. So I crawled on my belly, my fur dragging on the dirt. Long reaching steps, like a panther stalking, my mouth open now gasping for breath, tasting the acrid smoke from the vehicles. The owl woman seemed to be in front of me, guiding me with the power of her voice, teaching me to wait for gaps in the traffic when it was possible to run, low to the ground. Each time a lorry came I lay flat and clung to the road while the huge grey wheels trundled past.

At last I reached the slip road and the welcome softness of the grass. Had it not been for the owl woman constantly telling me to move on, I would have collapsed and probably died. 'You must get away from the road, Timba,' she kept saying. 'Get back into the clean air of the forest. Find some water, and rest.' I wondered how she knew I was in trouble.

It was dark when I reached the soothing canopy of trees. The damp moss had never felt so beautiful. I licked the moisture from leaves and grass. I wanted to wash, but my fur tasted poisonous, so I drifted into a deep sleep, only vaguely aware that rain was falling, cleansing me.

When I woke I remembered the owl woman helping me. She wasn't there now, but she'd said, 'Before long you will meet me again.' Did she mean meet her in my memory, or for real?

My fur was soaking wet. Cold, but clean! And I could breathe again. I stood up and stretched.

The longing to go home overwhelmed me. To hear

Angie's voice and have her brushing me so caringly, to see Leroy's bright smile and hear him say, 'Hello, Timba.' I loved my humans. What they did for me was awesome, and I enjoyed giving in return. It was an easy kind of giving . . . purring and entertaining and comforting.

I seriously considered turning back, across the miles of fields and lanes, through that nightmare maze of streets. Could I find my way?

Thoroughly miserable, I crawled into the solid arms of an ancient oak and found a dry place, protected by over-hanging branches. I stayed there for most of the day, occasionally bothering to open my eyes and watch the sparkle of raindrops over the white sky.

The creatures of the forest were disappearing from my life. Winter sent them deep into the earth to sleep, and my sensitive pads told me where they were. Hungry, I cir-cled the mouse holes and waited, but only the odd one popped out at the zenith of the day. I became dependent on the starlings. If they didn't come, I had nothing.

I was getting thinner. My fur felt loose, and so did my bones. My whiskers drooped and I no longer had the energy to play.

My telepathic 'chat line' to Vati seemed dead. Gloomily I speculated that Vati had actually died. Had he gone home to the spirit world, leaving me alone, the last of Solomon's kittens? Was I too late?

But there was a voice in my mind. Why did I keep ignoring it? It was insistent. 'Timba. Timba. Where are you, Timba?' Suddenly I came alive. I listened, not with my ears, but with my spirit.

'Timba. Timba,' the voice called huskily. Then it cried, and it prayed. Who was praying for me in that gruff voice? I sat up. My whiskers twitched, and my wet fur quivered as if an electric current had shot through me.

Leroy!

Was he searching in the forest? There was no smell of him, no running footsteps. He wasn't there. Leroy was talking to me by telepathy. My heart leapt with hope.

'I know you're not dead, Timba,' Leroy was saying. 'Angie and I made posters and put them up everywhere. We are searching for you every day, and Angie taught me to meditate so I can talk to you. I'm talking to you now. Are you listening, Timba? I miss you, Timba.'

I was listening. My spirits lifted, and I sent a message back. 'I've gone to find Vati. It's a long journey, but I will come home one day soon. Hang in there, Leroy.'

I sensed that he was crying hard. Had he got my message? Momentarily the crying stopped, and he said, 'Don't forget the White Lion, Timba, and the lion in the sky. He's made of stars and he's in the south.'

The lion in the sky! Something clicked in my mind, and I remembered a starry night in the garden when

Angie had shown Leroy the constellation of Leo, and on his paw was one of the brightest stars in the universe. Leroy had nearly burst with excitement, and every starry night he'd carried me into the garden and we'd faced south to find the star lion in the sky.

I yawned and stretched, and padded out into the glade. The rain had stopped. The magic was back. Between the bare trees I saw a blue-bright star. Was that the star on Leo's paw?

I walked towards that star, and my tail was up for the first time in weeks. The tiny beings of light glimmered in the wet grass, lighting the way for me, their eyes winking from the darkest places. I walked a different way out of the glade. I paused and felt the energy with my pads, the way the Spirit Lion had taught me. It was strong. A definite subterranean tingle. Mindfully I followed it between the trees, and came out on a long straight track, leading south towards the star.

I had found a golden road.

Chapter Fifteen

CROSSING THE BRIDGE

In the morning I was on the golden road, the easiest journey so far. I relaxed and followed its arrow-straight track which cut through the forest, uphill and downhill. It wasn't visibly golden. The 'gold' was a kind of song, deep in the earth, a song that tickled my pads with its own particular frequency. It reminded me of the way Graham sang one note for a long time and the glass and china rang with it for an even longer time.

Vati had told me certain notes were healing. So why wasn't he being healed now, in Graham's house? I knew the answer. Vati had closed down. He didn't eat, he didn't purr, he didn't play. Vati was like a frozen cat. Dangerously close to the point of no return. The thought drove me on, even when I was tired.

Rain had plumped domes of moss to springy softness under my paws. In places there were clear, shallow pools of water that tasted good and rinsed the dust from my pads. Altogether a paw-restoring experience. I began to feel kittenish and joyful again. The winter sun glinted on my whiskers, and warmed my back as I reached the top of the first hill where a group of deer were lying in the sun.

In places the track plunged downhill steeply and became a sunken road with high banks and overhanging ferns. The magic was there, and the tiny beings of light watched me with eyes that gleamed like raindrops.

On the third hill, my fur bushed out suddenly. I sensed danger, and couldn't identify what it was. I sat close to an oak tree, ready to climb into the safety of its branches if I needed to escape.

What spooked me was a change in the earth energy of the track. Something intrusive, a coarse thud-thudding vibration. Footsteps! Men, with heavy, stealthy boots, invading the forest. I could smell them, a leathery, fusty, smoky tang, and I could smell dogs too. Silent dogs, quivering with excitement.

Two rabbits shot past me, closer than a rabbit would normally come to a cat, and fled up the track, their tails bobbing. Wood pigeons with their loud, flappy wings were flying out of the trees in a panic. The deer sped past, scudding as if blown by the wind, their dark eyes afraid. Bewildered, I stayed by the oak tree, watching more and more creatures fleeing.

When I identified the smell of fear, I climbed the oak tree and crouched up there.

The first gunshot was so close that I nearly fell out of the tree in fright. It was followed by a volley of shooting, the bangs so loud that the shock of them jolted the delicate bones of my skull. My ears hurt and hurt and I began to tremble all over. I wished I'd found a safe hole, not this very public oak tree.

More shots, and more, and to my horror I saw a pheasant falling out of the sky, somersaulting horribly, its bright wings flailing. It crashed to the floor close to my tree, and then, even worse, a brown-and-white dog came leaping through the bracken, its tail wagging manically. With elaborate care it picked up the dying bird and carried it away.

The shooting went on and on. Death had come to the wood; the wild creatures who had made it their home were being blown out of the sky. Terrified and upset, I clung to the oak tree and tried not to move. Two men came striding up the track, and I smelled blood. Hanging from their belts were dead pheasants and dead rabbits, swinging limp and upside down, their feet cruelly tied together.

What if they did that to me? The dogs had smelled me. One of them ran round and round the tree, looking up at me and barking.

'What's up there?' The two men stopped under the tree. They peered up at me. I saw the glint of their eyes and their auras were a grubby red.

'It's a cat!' said the younger man, and his eyes narrowed. 'Bloody feral cats. I hate 'em.' He raised his gun and pointed it at me. I stared down at him. He clicked something and his eyes squinted along the shining metal at me.

'No!' cried the other man, and he raised his arm and knocked the gun sideways. 'Don't shoot the poor devil. He might be someone's lost cat.'

I heard kindness in the voice of this leathery man who had dead birds and rabbits hanging from his belt. I did what came naturally to me. I meowed at him. He looked pleased. 'There you are, he's friendly,' he said. 'Feral cats do not meow at people.' I meowed again, louder. I wanted to tell him how frightened I was, and how I was a cat on a journey.

'What are you doing so far from home, puss?' he asked. 'Are you lost?'

His concern touched my heart and I did an extended-meow which echoed into the tree. At the same time I eyeballed the dog who whined and retreated behind his master's legs. Once I'd done that, I wanted to make contact with this man who shot birds but had a heart. I worked my way down to a lower branch and walked along it, nicely, with my tail up.

'My missus would love you,' he said, and even though I was tatty and had burrs in my fur, he added, 'Aren't you beautiful?'

My spirits soared. This man was going to help me, I knew it. The words of the Spirit Lion came back to me. Be smart, he'd said. We touched noses, and I had him.

'You need a bit of TLC, old fella,' he said, and turned to the younger man who'd been going to shoot me. 'You take the dogs down and put them in the truck. I'll bring the cat, if he'll come.'

'You're not seriously going to catch a scruffy old thing like that, Alf,' protested the younger man, clipping a lead onto Alf's dog. 'Look at him. He's a flea bag.'

Alf sighed. 'It's payback time,' he said, patting the orange-red plumage of the dead pheasants that hung from his belt. 'You should try it some time.'

'You're an old softie.' The young man shrugged and set off, laden with his dead birds and his guns. 'See ya.'

Alf sat down heavily at the foot of the oak tree. He unclipped the dead pheasants and laid them on the grass. The gunman's footsteps faded, and peace settled back into the forest. Tiny movements restarted in the leaves and branches, a robin hopping, the twitch of a mouse's whiskers as he peeped from his hole in the grass. A green woodpecker flew down into the turf and stabbed at an ants' nest with his red-rimmed beak.

Alf didn't move. He didn't invite me down or look at me. He just sat, with his blue eyes on the distant hills and trees. He didn't shoot the woodpecker, but seemed to be enjoying his company.

Observing Alf from my branch, I saw that his aura was not such a grubby red colour now. It was filling with light, the kind of light a wise old soul would have around him ... blue, white and gold. He looked up at me. 'You coming down, puss?' he asked, and waited until I felt confident that the guns and dogs had gone and we were alone on the golden road. Cautiously I climbed down, eager for a cuddle with Alf. He was the first human I'd been close to for weeks.

I stepped carefully around the dead pheasants and put an exploratory paw on Alf's knee. A smile glistened in his eyes. 'Come on then,' he said, and patted his heart where he wanted me to sit. I crept up his tweedy jacket and arranged myself, stretching out, resting my chin over his sturdy old heart so that he could feel my purring. I wanted to cry like Leroy. After my long, lonely journey, it was such a relief to be close to another being.

'Oh ... you're a healing cat,' he murmured and his hand stroked and stroked my fur, giving me a beautiful head-to-tail massage. We were healing each other. He didn't care that my fur was in such a state. He loved me for who I was. Timba.

Alf stroked the dead pheasants with his other hand, his eyes sad. 'Sometimes I wish I hadn't shot 'em,' he confided. 'Sometimes I wonder if, when I die, they'll all be waiting for me at the pearly gates . . . all those birds I shot.'

My greatest gift, as a cat, is unconditional love, so I turned the purring up a notch and, when Alf looked down at me, I did a cat smile right into his soul. Then Alf said something amazing.

'I tell you what, puss, since you're so loving . . . I'm going to drive you across the bridge and take you home to my missus. Will you come?'

I felt like royalty as Alf drove me down from the forest across the bridge, despite sharing his magnificent car with some dead pheasants. They were dumped in the back and I sat on the front seat. Alf didn't seem to care that he hadn't got a cat cage for me. He asked me to sit still, and I did. The car was quiet and high up off the road so it didn't vibrate like Angie's car.

This time the river crossing wasn't so scary. I'd watched the bridge from the hills at night when it was all lights, and nobody fell in the river. The water was so far below that it seemed we were flying across the sky like the starlings I'd envied. I thought of Vati, and felt he would be proud of me for getting myself a lift. Smart cat!

After the bridge, Alf drove on over the next hill, and the next, and my heart leapt when I saw the tall metal tower that Leroy had wanted to climb. In the dark afternoon, it had a light flashing at the top. It would guide me, night and day, nearer and nearer to Vati.

My intention was to say goodbye, nicely, to Alf when he let me out of the car. Then I'd run on, across the blue-green countryside towards the metal tower. Surely my journey would soon come to an end.

It didn't work out like that. Alf swung the car into a yard with straw and chickens. He picked me up and carried me in his arms to the open door of a house.

Immediately my fur started to bristle, and a voice rang through my mind. 'Don't go in there, Timba.' It was insistent, and it was the voice of the Spirit Lion. I wanted a meal so badly. Something easy and tasty on a plate. I wanted a fire to warm my belly on that chilly day with the twilight deepening over a land that was strange to me. I deserved a bit of comfort. So I clung to Alf's shoulder as he carried me inside. A woman was sitting in a chair by the fire, knitting, but I hardly saw her.

I froze, and dug my claws into Alf's jacket.

A fox was looking at me. A real fox with his eyes glassy

and his teeth bared. He wasn't moving, but I swear his fur was bristling and his black nose smelling me.

'Don't worry about him,' said Alf. 'He's been there twenty years. I call him Bert. Don't worry, he's only stuffed.'

Stuffed? I didn't dare move in case the fox leapt down and savaged me.

'Oh what a lovely cat!' I heard the woman saying, but I heard her through a glaze of terror. It wasn't just the fox. All over the walls were the glassy-eyed heads of creatures, a stag, a hare, and more foxes.

I couldn't stand it.

With a thrust of my back legs I escaped from Alf's grip, and landed on the floor. In my terror I hadn't noticed where the exit was, and I ran through an open door into another room. On the floor was something even more horrific: it made my back go up and my eyes turn black with fright.

'Leave him. He'll get used to it,' I heard Alf say.

If Angie had been there, she would have screamed.

Stretched out in the middle of the room was an enormous tiger skin, lying flat with the beautiful colours glowing. At the far end was its head. Compelled to see its eyes, I inched my way round it, my back arched, my ears flat. And when I saw the tiger's face close up with its gleaming teeth and outraged golden eyes, I hissed and growled. The tiger didn't react. Like the fox, it had been dead for years. Overwhelming grief was for ever locked into its hard glass eyes.

I looked sadly at its paws. The sensitive pads were gone, and the claws. Only the skin with its lush, richly coloured fur was splayed across the carpet, never moving. And it was a cat. It hadn't been rescued and pampered like me. Why? I wondered. The question ruffled my fur like a freezing wind.

Alf was standing in the doorway, watching me. 'It's OK, puss,' he said, 'it's dead ... been dead for years ... it's a rug now, you can walk on it ... look.' He strode forward and placed his muddy boots on the tiger's beautiful coat, where the colours were so achingly bright. I was appalled.

My terror became a fragment of the global sadness that engulfed me, along with the bewilderment. How could humans be so disrespectful? I glanced at Alf, and saw guilt deep down in his soul, simmering, seeking a way out. 'I didn't shoot him,' he said to me. 'Bought him, years ago, at an auction. Splendid, isn't he? We love him.'

Love him! I couldn't stay in that house for another minute.

Running scared and low to the ground, I escaped through the open door, and saw the woman, who held a dish of cat food in her hand. 'Here you are, puss,' she crooned. I flattened my ears and shot past her into the yard. Chickens flew everywhere, and the dog chased me triumphantly as I streaked across the yard. I ran hard, into unknown country, high hills covered in heather and gorse. The sky was starless and alive with big soft snowflakes, the first snow of winter. Alf's words rang in my head. 'It's OK, puss.'

It wasn't OK. It wasn't. It never would be.

Day after day I ran on through the snow, my paws wet and icy cold. Hunger ached in my belly. Food was hard to find ... the mice were tucked up sensibly under the ground, and the birds I stalked saw me too easily, a black cat against the snow. I was getting even thinner and weaker.

When I reached the metal tower, I was exhausted. Its winking light had guided me on starless nights and cloudy days. How long since I'd eaten? I didn't know, couldn't remember, and didn't actually care.

The snow had made a thick crust over the gorse and heather, like a roof. Once I found a way in, there was a different world, a twilight of roots and dry branches, dimly lit under the crystal covering of snow. It was surprisingly warm and spacious, and lots of creatures were getting on with their lives in there: mice, slow-worms and hedgehogs. Grateful for such perfect shelter, I stayed under there for days. Long days when I didn't see the sky, but if I listened I could hear the snowflakes softly landing on the canopy, making it thicker and thicker. I knew when the sun was shining by the shafts of yellow light beaming through cracks. It tempted me out.

The morning was icy blue and clear, a bitter wind singing through the tall tower. I found shelter under an overhanging clump of bracken, a dry haven the snow hadn't reached. I dozed and slept through the morning, aware that sleep was not restoring me. I needed food.

After the experience with Alf, I'd chosen to avoid villages, and stay in the open countryside. But now, hunger drove me down over the crisp snow to a row of houses. I mustn't get caught. I waited until dark, then raided two of the cat flaps, hungrily eating what those lucky cats had left, mostly cheap fishy stuff and hard little rings of dried cat food which took too long to eat when I was thieving.

I felt better, but missed being able to sit and have a leisurely wash in a warm place.

I inspected my paws which were sore from the wedges of hard snow stuck between the pads. Sitting under the heather I managed to wash my face, but trying to clean my thick fur was impossible, and the hairballs made me sick. I felt like giving up. It would have been so easy to turn up on a friendly doorstep with my tail up, and get invited in to sit by a warming fire.

At noon that day, I tried to talk to Vati. 'I'm not far away, but it's so hard. I'm cold and hungry, and my fur is in a mess. Couldn't you come to meet me?' I asked. Silence. The black, haunted eyes looked blankly into my soul. Nothing had changed. 'Why can't I reach you?' I sent the question, but it hung in the air unanswered.

And then, white as snow, the Spirit Lion padded back into my life. This time he didn't lie down and wrap me in his love. He simply asked me to follow him through the snow. I trotted after him, focusing on his shining light, and he took me to a ridge where the snowdrifts twinkled in the sun.

'Look, Timba,' he said. 'You're nearly there.'

I sat beside him, gazing at the land below the hills, and my heart leapt when I saw that it was green. Green like summer. There was no snow down there!

Eagerly I ran to sit between his paws, but he wouldn't let me rest. 'Look for the stone tower,' he said, and immediately I saw it, far in the distance, floating like an island in the hazy landscape. My pads tingled. That same sacred energy, deep in the earth, was there, even in the snow. It cut through the land like a silver sword, and right at the end I could see Vati, sitting in his barrel ... waiting for me, his eyes just a breath away from a sparkle.

'You must go now,' the Spirit Lion said. 'More snow is coming, thick snow that will cover the green earth for many weeks. You are weak, Timba. Go now ... NOW ... while you still have strength.'

He was trying to tell me I could die in the snow if I didn't move fast. I dumped the depression and the despair, and raced down the hill, through the blue shadows of hedges and gates, across lanes and through copses. By the end of the day I was down there in the green grass, and there were still mice around!

The golden road became a real road and this time it was raised on a high bank as it led through the levels. Deep ditches and knobbly willow trees lined the route and there was no traffic. Only the occasional loud tractor bounced past while I hid in the dead clumps of reeds. A few fields away was a busy road with lorries and cars.

When I paused to look back at the snow-covered hills with the metal tower, slate-coloured clouds were rolling, and the north wind howled through the willow trees. The blizzard was chasing me. The Spirit Lion was still with me, a flare of light brighter than the white snow. He was watching me, and that was comforting. Encouraged, I ran on, searching for signs of home. I still thought of Graham's house as 'home'. It had been my first real home and I loved it.

The longing and the ache of loneliness kept me moving, imagining the blissful sleep I would have by the fire, the plate of Whiskas rabbit in the cosy kitchen. And the welcome! The joy of being in Graham's huge arms again, the warm comfort of the sofa, the sparkle in Vati's eyes as he welcomed me. The touch and smell of my beloved brother.

I was SO looking forward to being home that I ran faster and faster, only stopping to shake the wet snow off my fur. My paws stung with cold, and I felt wretchedly tired. But Vati was close. I could feel him.

I crossed a field into a lane. Everything was different and muffled under the fresh snow. I followed one of the hard, slippery wheel tracks, finding it easier on the hard-packed, yellowish snow.

With one paw in the air, I paused by a gateway to listen. All around me was the muted patter of snowflakes, and the crack of twigs as the north wind tore through the trees. A child's voice crying. A woman's voice. And then . . . an old familiar sound that told me I was home.

'Ah, ah, ah, ah, ah, ah, ah, AH.'

I belted across the lawn with snow flying from my fur, and charged through the dear old cat flap.

And in that moment I was a kitten again, full of hope and unconditional love. I shook myself, put my tail up, and swanned into the lounge.

Chapter Six

YOU SMELL

Chapter Sixteen

YOU SMELLY OLD CAT

Vati was hunched in the corner of the sofa. His fur had lost its gloss, and his hip bones stuck out either side of his spine. His face was pixie-like and thin, his eyes black and frightened. He saw me, but he didn't come to greet me. He didn't move at all.

I jumped onto the sofa, my fur and paws soaking wet. Did Vati even know it was snowing? Why wasn't he sitting in the window watching? I was overjoyed to see my brother again, and happy to be in the warm house which had once been my home. I wanted to give Vati lots of love and healing, so I immediately set about licking him, rubbing cheeks and purring. He didn't respond.

'I'm here now,' I said. 'I'll take care of you.' Telling

him about my long journey didn't seem appropriate. Vati was traumatised, and maybe I was the only person who could bring him out of it. Words were pretty useless, so I purred and made a fuss of Vati. He lay there unmoving, like a china cat. I looked at his eyes, and they had a flat frowny line over the top lids. In the end I lay down and leaned against him, wrapping my tail round his back and letting my loud purr fill both our bodies.

Vati did look at me then, hesitantly, as if he didn't dare to move. Then a chubby little girl toddled into the room. She squealed with delight when she saw me, and ran to stroke me. 'Big new pussy cat!' she called, and Lisa appeared from the kitchen.

She gasped when she saw me on the sofa with Vati. 'Don't touch him, Heidi,' she snapped and pulled the little girl away. Then she screamed at me. 'GET OUT, you smelly old cat!'

Astonished, I looked at her and purred. I even gave her a cat smile. But she went berserk, picked up a newspaper and swiped me as if I was a wasp. 'Get OUT!' she screamed. 'OUT...!'

I didn't move, but I was shocked at being hit like that. Surely she hadn't meant it. Had she?

She shrieked for Graham. 'There's a dreadful smelly old cat on the sofa, and it won't move.'

I assumed Graham would come in and be pleased to see me. We'd been buddies, I thought proudly.

'Sorry, love. I'm late now and it's snowing. I've got to go,' he called from the hall. 'You deal with it. See you later. Bye.'

'MEN,' said Lisa angrily. 'NO, Heidi . . . leave the cat alone. You are not to touch it. NO.'

Heidi began to cry like Leroy, and Lisa picked up the screaming child and dumped her in a round playpen in the kitchen. When she came back she had a broom in her hand.

'OUT,' she insisted and tried to sweep me off the sofa! I was appalled, and a bit frightened. I wasn't going to leave Vati now that I'd travelled so many miles to find him. I crouched against the back of the sofa, shut my eyes, and clung on with my claws.

'You're wet and disgusting. WILL YOU GO OUT!' Lisa screamed. 'I don't want you here. Have you got that, you stinking old feral cat? I don't want you.'

Vati didn't move. He seemed resigned to this sort of behaviour. I looked steadily at Lisa's eyes and saw that she was afraid to pick me up or touch me. She was making a pantomime with a broom to scare me out.

I stayed put, and felt a glimmer of something resembling gratitude from Vati. He needed me. I had come to be his support cat. I radiated that thought to Lisa, and when she found I wasn't going to let her chase me out, she gave up and threw the broom against the wall. 'You wait till Graham gets home,' she warned. 'He'll deal with you,' and she took Heidi upstairs.

Meanwhile, Vati had gone back into his shell. The moment of response I'd worked so hard for had been crushed by Lisa's hysteria. I'd have to start all over again, coaxing and encouraging my frozen brother.

First I needed to eat, so I headed for the kitchen where I found a cat dish with the dreaded dried food in it. So boring. I needed something succulent and sustaining, so I picked at the fridge door with both paws, pulling and pulling until it swung open. I stood there, sniffing the cornucopia of delicious smells. I pulled out a slab of cheese, but it was tightly sealed in plastic, so I left it on the floor for later. Standing up on my hind legs I inspected the next shelf, and pulled at some tin foil with my teeth. It floated, crackling, to the floor. Under it was a plate of cooked chicken. WOW! I meowed at Vati, but he still sat there like a china cat.

I pulled some chunks out onto the floor, and tucked into the best meal I'd had for months. I ate until I was satisfied, then picked up a really choice piece of chicken and carried it through to Vati. A fleeting look of surprise passed through his eyes. He sniffed the chicken, and gave it a lick. Then he pushed it away with his nose. It fell on the carpet and he resumed his frozen cat pose.

I felt like swiping him.

Instead, I sat beside him, washing and purring. Then I wrapped myself around him and drifted into sleep, warm and comfortable for the first time since leaving my home with Angie and Leroy. The north wind was blowing snow against the windows, and Graham's mother's clock still ticked and chimed. I could hear the beat of my heart and the anxious beat of Vati's. We'd always slept intertwined. Now it was me doing the twining, and Vati sitting there like a stone.

Surprisingly, it was my sleeping and my silent presence that slowly began to unlock Vati. There was a magic moment when I felt him relax against me. He snuggled into my fur with a little sigh, as if he'd waited through a long hard time for the comfort of my brother love. Half asleep, I did a mini purr-meow to encourage him, and I felt his paws reach out and slowly wrap themselves around me.

The magic of the forest seemed there as we slept deeply. The tiny beings of light had somehow stayed with me, and blessed me. Now they clustered over both of us, and the warm radiance of my aura flooded into Vati's pale thin rim of light, energising and restoring him. I didn't have to do anything. Only love. And love brings light in all its myriad forms.

231

Loving Vati back to life was the easiest, most beautiful and nurturing experience. After the long hard journey, it was a sacred gift of contentment, and I knew that, no matter what the humans did, they couldn't take that away from us. We were twin souls, Timba and Vati, named after the White Lions who had come to save the world.

I woke briefly and saw Vati nestled into me, his face turned upwards in a smile, and I asked for time. Time for the healing to be complete, before the humans came back and tore our lives apart. I longed for Angie and Leroy. Here, with Graham and Lisa, I wasn't sure what would happen.

Lisa had called me a smelly old cat! Maybe she was only seeing my matted fur, not ME. It hurt. A lot. But I tried not to think about it. I focused on remembering Vati. He'd been such a bright spirit, such fun to play with, and full of mysterious knowledge. He was a hypersensitive cat, a gift of pure gold to the human race ... so what had happened to him? I still didn't know.

I was glad it was Graham, and not Lisa, who came in at the end of the afternoon, stamping the snow from his shoes and leaving them on the mat. He padded into the lounge, and recognised me immediately.

'Timba!' He stared down at me, and I gave him a cat smile and a purr-meow. I didn't want to disturb Vati.

'I don't believe it!' Graham said incredulously. 'How did you get here, Timba? Surely . . . surely you didn't find your way from South Wales!'

I did one of my yes-meows, and because Graham knew me so well, he understood. He sat down on the floor and looked at me with respect and compassion. Very welcome, after the way Lisa had treated me! I wanted to touch noses with Graham, but I felt committed to keeping still for Vati's sake. I appreciated Graham bringing his face close to me so that we could touch noses. I felt emotional, so did he, judging by the tears in his eyes. He stroked my fur tenderly, his fingers touching the burrs and tangles. 'You ARE in a sorry state, Timba,' he said. 'And you came through all that snow! Poor fellow. And how did you get across the river? Oh Timba! All that way. What a brave, clever cat.'

Graham was talking to me so kindly, I wanted to cry. I kept doing my yes-meows in response. He looked at Vati who was still curled like a seashell, his chin upwards, looking blissful as he snuggled into my thick fur. 'Vati needed you,' Graham said, 'and you knew, didn't you, Timba? Poor little Vati. I feel so, so guilty . . . I wish . . .'

He was going to tell me what had happened. I tensed, hearing Lisa coming down the stairs. She opened the door cautiously, peering through. 'Have you got rid of it?' she demanded.

Graham looked sheepish, but he kept stroking me.

'Lisa, this is Timba,' he said. 'He's found his way here, alone, from South Wales for goodness' sake! Two hundred miles.'

'I don't care, Graham. He's DISGUSTING. I want him out of our house.'

Graham kept his hand on me protectively. 'I am not going to chuck Timba out in the snow,' he said steadily. 'He can't help being a bit scruffy after a journey like that.'

'A bit scruffy!' Lisa looked at me angrily. 'He stinks to high heaven, and he's got fleas, and he's made the sofa such a mess, Graham, and what about Heidi?'

'What about her? She's OK, isn't she? Is she in bed?'

'She's asleep, thank God. Otherwise she'd be all over that filthy cat. Graham, it's a health hazard, and I want it out.'

'You're overreacting, darling. I repeat ... I am not going to chuck him out. He's staying right here until Angie can collect him.'

'Have you phoned her?'

'No ... I've only been here for five minutes. I'll phone Angie in the fullness of time.'

'The fullness of time! And meanwhile our home ... your daughter's home ... is being messed up and ... oh my God ... is that a piece of chicken on the floor?'

'Where?'

'You're nearly sitting on it.'

Graham turned and saw Vati's piece of chicken where he had dropped it. He picked it up and put it on the sofa.

'Don't put it on the sofa! It's made enough mess on the carpet. We'll have germs everywhere. Do you want Heidi to get salmonella?'

Graham refused to get ruffled. He waggled the piece of chicken and winked at me. 'Who raided the fridge then?' he teased. 'Tut tut! You know what, Lisa? This cat can actually open the fridge. He's brought Vati a meal. Isn't that sweet?'

'Stop being so infuriating.' Lisa's aura was hanging in shreds. She stamped her foot and yelled at Graham. 'OK . . . either you sort these cats or I'm packing my bag, taking Heidi to stay with my mum. Right now.' She turned and went out, slamming the door and making Vati jump. I purred into his ear and gave him a lick on the top of his head, and he settled back into sleep.

Graham sighed and rolled his eyes.

'I'd better ring Angie,' he said. 'She'll be ecstatic.'

In the deep of the night I found out what was wrong with Vati, and it was worse than anything I could have imagined.

As always, I awoke at midnight. I heard Graham's

mother's clock chiming all of its chimes. I disentangled myself from Vati and climbed up to my favourite windowsill. The snowstorm was over, and a yellow moon shone on the silent snow. Each twig and branch of the apple tree was encrusted with glitter.

It occurred to me that, in the morning, I wouldn't have to be on a journey. I was free to eat and play! First, I raided the fridge again and found the rest of the chicken. I took the best, most succulent chunk to Vati. This time he looked at me, and he did eat a little bit. Once he'd done that, he ate more, then he sat up and stared at me. I stared back and saw that he wanted me to notice the pain in his mystic eyes.

'So what happened?' I asked.

Silently Vati held out his front paw to me. It looked strange, and there was a sense of heat and pain. I sniffed it, then Vati silently held out the other one. It was the same.

'What happened?' I asked again.

I waited, and Vati began to cry and cry, the way a very distressed cat cries, in little squeaks and growls. His pain was beyond words, and it wasn't physical pain, from an accident or illness. Vati had been assaulted. His beautiful paws, such a tender part of this sensitive little cat, had been deliberately damaged.

My dreams of playing in the snow with Vati disappeared under a black cloud. I let him cry, and sat close, licking and comforting him as best I could. When he had cried enough, he did manage to tell me the appalling truth.

'They took my claws away,' he said, and flexed his toes so that I could understand. His magnificent claws had gone. Just gone! And to Vati it felt as if his whole life had been ruined. He was no longer joyful and free to play and climb. He couldn't defend himself. And he felt violated.

No wonder I had sensed that Vati was willing himself to die.

'Why?' I asked, devastated.

'Heidi pulled my tail, really hard,' he said. 'It hurt all along my spine, and she wouldn't stop it, so I scratched her. Then Lisa got the broom and chased me outside, and the next day when I was eating my breakfast, she grabbed me and put me in the cat cage. She took me to the vet and told him she wanted me de-clawed. Rick refused to do it, so she drove me to another vet and he did it . . . put me to sleep, and when I woke up my front paws were burning with pain. I couldn't walk, and I couldn't balance. I couldn't believe what they'd done to me.'

'That's terrible,' I said, and felt his pain intensely in my own paws, and in my heart.

'And it's for ever,' Vati said.

I felt powerless and angry. Was this what the Spirit Lion

had felt? Shocked beyond words at the cruelty imposed by humans. I seriously considered taking Vati off into the wild. We would travel on the golden road and live in the forest, in secret, away from humans, for the rest of our lives. I pledged never to leave my brother again.

The instant I thought about him, the Spirit Lion appeared. Vati's eyes grew luminous and round and his aura brightened around his sleek fur. We were lying side by side, and the lion cupped us both in velvet paws. A lion purrs differently to a cat, only on the out-breath, but the purr is loud, like a drum roll. We snuggled together in the bliss of his light. I sensed that Vati had not purred since losing his claws, but he did now, and hearing his economical little purr blending with my loud one was calming and uplifting.

'You are not powerless, Timba,' breathed the Spirit Lion, 'because you can love, and it's never too late for love.' He looked at Vati tenderly. 'You two cats have a destiny. You must stay together now, but not in the wild. Vati needs care. He can't get his claws back, but he can learn to live again with your encouragement, Timba ... something you're so good at.'

I glowed with joy. To be praised at such a time was brilliant.

'Both you cats can teach and inspire,' added the Spirit Lion, and he showed me Leroy who was far away in

South Wales, awake and at the window watching that same yellow moon on the snow. 'Humans cannot teach Leroy. He has encrypted knowledge and courage to follow his dreams. He needs love in abundance, for he has chosen a lonely path. Every day of his life he faces bullying and hostility from those who seek to disempower him, yet he keeps a cheerful heart.'

'So what can we teach him?' I asked.

'Unconditional love. Always and for ever. And from the source, all good intentions flow. Power and courage and understanding. Unconditional love is the beginning of healing and the gateway to true knowledge.'

The Spirit Lion gave a huge sigh. 'Remind him ... and Angie ... to have fun, for humour is the bridge over troubled waters.'

I felt him vanishing into the crystal silence of the snow. 'Stay together,' he whispered, and left us, curled close in Vati's corner of the sofa.

At first light, Lisa tiptoed downstairs and threw me a look of pure hatred. She came towards me, her hands engulfed in a pair of yellow rubber gloves. Then she changed her mind, and went into the kitchen. She slammed the fridge closed, took a roll of sticky tape from a drawer and taped the cat flap shut! She opened the door to the garden and cold air came in like smoke.

With her hands spread wide she approached me again. She was tense, and breathing fast, her eyes watching me. I got it. Lisa was going to grab me with those horrible yellow gloves, and chuck me out in the snow.

Vati sensed it too. He looked at Lisa and did the extended-meow. It was an appeal, straight from the heart. 'Don't take my brother away,' but Lisa kept coming. I dug myself in, pressed against the back of the sofa.

She grabbed me, but I hung on, hooking my claws into the upholstery. She pulled and pulled, but I resisted. She was panting now. 'Come on . . . come on. You are going OUT,' she muttered, and I did something I'd never done before. I growled at her like a dog, and glared into her frustrated eyes. Vati joined in, growling and making a terrible fish face.

'You stubborn old bugger,' she ranted, and let me go. She was shaking all over. She went back into the kitchen, tore the tape off the cat flap and flung the yellow rubber gloves into a cupboard.

Vati and I looked at each other triumphantly. Round one . . . to Timba and Vati!

Chapter Seventeen

HEALING THE HURT

'Why do people keep calling me old?' I asked Vati. 'I'm a young cat.'

'It's your fur,' he said tactfully. 'It needs a good sort-out.'

'Angie would know what to do,' I said, and we both looked serious. It occurred to me that Vati looked better and was responding to me now. I remembered what the Spirit Lion had said about fun. 'We're getting too serious,' I said, and looked around for the catnip mouse. Lisa had gone upstairs, so I got down and found it tucked away in a little basket under the window. Pleased, I took it over to Vati and put it under his nose. Light flashed through his eyes, just for a second, and I waited for him to play with it. Instead, he pushed it away and bunched his paws under himself again, setting his face back into frozen mode.

So I opted for a mad half-hour on my own ... in this house I knew so well. Maybe Vati would join in, I thought, flinging the catnip mouse into the air. I took it over to Graham's shoes and stuffed it into the toe. Then I had fun getting it out and chased it around. I even got bold and took it to the top of the stairs and dropped it through the banisters. I pretended not to notice Vati's eyes on me, with that fleeting light of interest flickering through them. He wanted to play. Give me a few days and I'll have him playing, I thought.

I got wilder and wilder, tearing up and down the stairs and over the back of the sofa, skidding along the kitchen floor and crumpling the rug that was in there. I found one of Heidi's teddy bears and gave it a beating. I got right on top of it and kicked it with my back legs. Then I grabbed it by one ear, skidded along the kitchen worktop with it, and dropped it in the washing-up bowl. I hadn't had so much fun for weeks.

But the sound of a door being opened upstairs sent me bounding back onto the sofa. I dug myself in, next to Vati. My eyes were wild and my fur itching like mad. I scratched furiously, scattering fluff all over the sofa.

It was Graham. Phew!

I wanted to tell him exactly how Lisa made me feel, how it had hurt to be called a smelly old cat at the end of a long, long journey, so I did an amplified extended-meow. He listened, and sat down beside us, smelling of shower gel and bundled in his cuddly blue towelling robe. 'Don't worry, Timba,' he said, 'I've been chucked out of bed to ring Angie . . . catch her before she goes to work.'

I stared into Graham's eyes and studied the strange mixture of kindliness and guilt. It was rare for me to do two amplified extended-meows . . . one was usually enough . . . but I wanted him to know how much Vati was suffering, so I did another one, and put my paw on Vati's bony little head.

'Oh dear . . . I know, I know, Timba,' Graham said. 'Vati is not a happy cat. I'll have to tell Angie. She'll go ballistic.'

He invited me onto his lap to listen to the phone call, but I was determined to stay close to Vati. We both listened to the sound of Angie's phone ringing.

'Hello, this is Angie.'

When I heard that beautiful, warm, expectant voice again, I was overwhelmed with joy. Vati was listening too, and his eyes shimmered green as he looked at me. Is this really happening? he was thinking. We sat up, side by side, gazing attentively into the phone. I half expected a plate of Whiskas rabbit to come whizzing down the line. And a brush. That's what Angie would have for me: a brush to heal my fur, and an angel cuddle to heal my soul.

'Graham!' she said brightly. 'Why so early?'

'I tried to get you last night,' he said.

'Parents' evening,' said Angie. 'It went on for ever. So come on . . . spill. Graham, it's not like you to ring at this time. Has somebody died?'

'No,' said Graham, and his eyes sparkled with pleasure at what he was going to tell her. 'Guess who turned up here?'

'Who?'

'Timba.'

'TIMBA! Surely not?'

'Yes, it's Timba. He's OK, here on the sofa right next to me.'

There was a brief silence. Then we heard the scream of joy that made Graham smile. Even Vati narrowed his eyes and gave a ghost of a cat smile. I could see how much Vati wanted Angie. He needed her healing love, desperately.

'But, Graham,' Angie said, 'Timba went missing last autumn . . . it's February now. Are you sure it's him?'

'One hundred per cent,' said Graham, and he stroked the top of my head. 'Purr for Angie.' He held the phone close to my face. I did yet another amplified extended-meow, and was rewarded with a second scream of joy.

'That sounds like Timba. It IS him. Oh my God! Oh wow . . . I can't stop crying. Oh Timba . . . you found your way down there . . . two hundred miles . . . oh you darling, darling, clever cat. I can't stop crying. Oh THANK YOU, UNIVERSE!'

Graham beamed from ear to ear. 'A long time since I've heard THAT,' he said.

'Is he really OK?' Angie asked. 'All his legs and tail . . . no injuries?'

'No. He's in full working order,' said Graham. 'His fur is a mess, and he was hungry . . . but he hasn't forgotten how to open the fridge.'

'I LOVE it!' Angie said. I wondered what she would say if she knew that Lisa had called me a smelly old cat. 'Hang on a minute, Graham . . . I've got to wake Leroy.' We listened and heard Angie's swift footsteps, and the squeak of Leroy's bedroom door. She didn't yell at him, but whispered, 'Wake up, Leroy. Fantastic news. You've got to wake up.'

There was a subterranean grunt of protest.

'Graham's got Timba. And he's OK.'

'Aw! Is that true, Angie? No kidding?'

'No kidding. Timba is BACK.'

We heard them bang their hands together and shout, 'YES!'

'Gimme the phone,' Leroy said, and then I heard another sound I'd longed for on my lonely journey. A scratchy voice saying, 'Hello, Timba.' I did purr-meows then, a whole stream of them. 'Where you been, Timba? I missed you. I cried lots,' Leroy said.

'He's kissing the phone,' Graham said, laughing at me.

I imagined Leroy's bright face. The ache in my heart had gone, and I felt the love from both my humans. I felt like the luckiest cat on the Planet.

'He's purring now.' Graham was still beaming from ear to ear, and he let me purr into the phone. I knew it had to be loud. That purr had to go rippling across the miles, over the shining river, through the dark forest, to reach my loved ones.

'Can you come and fetch him, Angie? Or shall I bring him up there?'

'Of course I'll come and fetch him. Wild horses wouldn't stop me,' Angie said. 'Thank goodness it's a Saturday. What's the snow like at your end?'

'It's thawing,' Graham said, looking at the window. I followed his gaze and saw the morning sun shining on melting crusts of crystal, diamond bright, sliding down the glass.

Graham didn't stop smiling until he saw Lisa, her spine straight like an icicle, her face stiff with hatred. We all looked at her, and the energy changed. I moved myself between her and Vati, and hooked my claws into her sofa. Smelly old cat, was I? Then a smelly old cat I'd be, proud and magnificent, and fierce.

No one, not even Angie, was going to separate me from Vati. So what would I do when she came to fetch me?

*

Graham tried to take me to the vet before Angie arrived. I didn't want to go, especially after what Vati had told me. Lisa might have me de-clawed too! So once again, I dug myself into the sofa, and as fast as Graham tried to unhook my claws, I clamped them in again.

'You really are being very difficult, Timba,' he said, exasperated. But when I looked at him and wailed plaintively, he got the message. 'I know, you don't want to leave Vati, do you? Well, he could come with us.' Vati threw Graham a withering look and went straight under the sofa. Graham sat down and put his head in his hands. 'My life is full of difficult cats ... and difficult women,' he complained, eyeing Lisa who was supervising from the doorway, with Heidi bright-eyed in her arms.

'Well, I am not ... repeat am not ... getting lunch for HER,' Lisa said, and I knew she meant Angie. Odd that Angie also referred to Lisa as HER. 'And I want a new sofa. Tomorrow.'

Graham persuaded the vet to come to us. It was Rick, and I remembered him. He was a radiant being of light. Even Vati came out to inspect him, and once he saw that Graham had put the cat cage away, he crept back into his corner of the sofa. Rick sat down on the sofa with his long legs stretched out. I arranged myself over his heart, and he didn't seem to mind my tatty fur. 'You are a loving old boy,' he said.

'He's only a young cat,' Graham said. 'And he's just been on a journey . . . two hundred miles . . . to find his brother. That's why his fur is such a mess.'

'It will have to be cut, and allowed to grow back,' said Rick, stroking me with his long translucent fingers. 'But I won't do that. I'll leave you a leaflet about long-furred cats, and I suggest Angie does that for him when she gets him home. We need to go one step at a time with Timba. He's had a huge trauma.'

Rick was a genius of a vet. A secret healer. He managed to love me and give me two injections which were over before I knew it. He put some drops on me to make the fleas go away, and put stuff in my ears to stop the ear mites, all the time loving me and talking to me.

When he had finished, he didn't just dump me, but let me stay stretched out on his body so he could feel my purr and my gratitude. Out of the corner of my eye I noticed Vati was sitting up and looking intently at Rick.

'So, what's wrong with this little cat?' he asked. 'Vati, is it?'

Graham looked guilty. 'My wife had him de-clawed,' he explained. 'He's a sensitive cat and he was a real personality. . . but it changed him. He's never been the same since. He doesn't play, he hardly eats . . . as you can see.'

Vati held out his paw to Rick, his green eyes shimmering with pain. The two men looked moved. Silently

Vati put his paw down and held out the other one. Rick took it gently and closed his hand around it. 'Poor Vati,' he murmured, and his hand shone with celestial light. It changed colour, from blazing white to soothing emerald green, bathing Vati's hurt paw in healing love.

We all sat respectfully still, for this was magic. Magic so rare and sensitive that it needed total peace in order to work. In those moments I heard the drip-drip of melting snow from the garden, the tick-tick of Graham's mother's clock, and my purring sending its ripples through the silence.

Rick closed his eyes, and seemed to be listening to something. The words came through, glimmering and slow, but strong, each one touching the pain that was knotted into the little cat's heart. Vati was alert and listening, soaking up the healing as if it were sunshine on his fur.

'We can't give you back your claws, Vati,' Rick said, 'but you can learn to walk again, and play again. You mustn't try to climb trees, but you can leap and run, and play with Timba.'

The light in Rick's hands changed to a powerful resonant blue, and he moved them gently to touch the little cat's head. 'Let go, Vati,' he said, 'let go of all the anger. Send it into the light and let it vanish for ever.' Vati gave a deep sigh and I saw the darkness leave his aura. 'It can no longer harm you,' Rick said. 'You are free.'

Sometimes I understood that certain things happen for a reason. It was meant to be. Rick was meant to be there, to heal Vati. And when Graham had tried to lift me from the sofa, I'd been given lion strength to resist. So Rick had come to the house, on his day off, he said, and given us his time.

I noticed Lisa, one arm holding Heidi and the other carefully wheeling a suitcase through the hall. I heard the click of car doors, and the businesslike whirr of her car as she left the house. For ever, said a voice in my mind. It's for ever.

'Do you mind if I hang around for an hour or so?' Rick asked. 'I'd like to finish this work I'm doing with Vati . . . and see Angie when she arrives.'

'Sure,' Graham said. 'I'll make some coffee.'

'No,' Rick said quietly. 'It's important that you sit here with me, Graham. Don't break this healing circle we've created for Vati. We need your energy.'

Graham rolled his eyes, as if he was going to say something scathing about 'mumbo-jumbo', but Rick looked at him with steel in his eyes. 'Will you hold Timba now?' he asked. 'I want to see if Vati will come to me.' Rick airlifted me to Graham's chest where I continued purring, and arranged myself so that I could see Vati.

Vati knew he was inside a bubble of magic. Moving gracefully, he slipped onto Rick's chest like a piece of

250

velvet. He lay gazing at Rick, his hurt paws stretched out. Graham's mother's clock went on ticking, the melting snow dripping, and I saw the stars come down. One soft bright star on each of Vati's paws, and a pure blue star for his mind.

Like the star lion in the sky.

The timing was perfect.

When the healing was complete, Vati jumped down and stretched. He put his tail up and wove himself around Graham's ankles. 'That's the first time he's had his tail up!' Graham said, and Vati meowed at him and headed for the kitchen.

'Don't give him that dried food,' Rick said. 'He needs something juicy.'

Graham opened two sachets of Whiskas and put them in a bowl for us to share. Vati ate ravenously, and we shared without growling, best friends and brothers.

Soon we were sitting side by side, gazing into the fire and appreciating its bright warmth, while Rick and Graham talked over coffee.

'How did you learn to do that kind of healing?' Graham asked. 'Spiritual healing, is it? I bet you didn't learn that at uni.'

'No, I didn't,' Rick said. 'A wonderful old lady taught me . . . Mrs Lanbrow.'

Sheila Jeffries

I did a purr-meow and stared at Rick. 'Yes, Timba . . . you remember her. She rescued you and brought you in when you were a kitten.'

'It certainly seems to work,' Graham said, frowning. 'I've never believed in all that stuff . . . but look at Vati now!'

My priority was to stay with Vati. I had made that perfectly clear. So what would happen when Angie came to collect me?

The sound of her car was bittersweet for me. The love, the ache of longing had stayed in my heart through my long lonely journey. I wanted Angie. I wanted Leroy. Yet now, as I sat expectantly looking at the door, my thoughts were tinged with anxiety. Even as those quick, beloved footsteps sounded, the idea of making a run for freedom came into my mind. But how would Vati survive in the wild without claws? Could I do the work of two cats? Protecting and feeding both of us, living for ever with matted fur and aching hunger, and a lonely heart?

'Don't do it, Timba. Don't even THINK about it.' The voice of the Spirit Lion boomed in my head. He was there, in the room with us. I could see his light as he prowled around, for a reason I had yet to discover.

'Come in, Angie,' Graham called, and stood up eagerly. He's still in love with her, I thought.

Leroy burst in, his eyes finding me immediately, his face

lighting up with passion. I did the loudest meow EVER and found myself trotting across the room with my tail up.

'TIMBA!'

Leroy couldn't speak. He picked me up and in wordless joy buried his face in my fur.

'Darling cat!' Leroy let me go and I climbed over to Angie, and wrapped my paws around her neck. I did a whole stream of purr-meows, and licked the tears from her face.

'Aren't you going to say it?' Graham asked, beaming.

'Say what?'

'Thank you, Universe,' he teased.

Angie smiled into his eyes. They looked at each other for a long moment. 'When I can stop crying,' Angie said, and Graham took THE HANKY from his top pocket and handed it to her. 'Oh dear ... I've missed this hanky too ... it's good to see you, Graham ... and, yes ... thank you, Universe!'

'Let me have Timba ... please, Angie,' Leroy said, and I went, purring, back to him and touched noses. Leroy had grown taller and stronger. His aura was huge, and he seemed quieter, more grown-up.

'You've had a long drive in the snow,' Graham said. 'Will you stay and have lunch? Lisa's not here, but we can have toast and soup, or something.'

'OK, thanks. Then we'll take Timba home,' Angie said,

and no one seemed to notice Vati who was sitting on the rug, watching everyone, his eyes lonely and anxious. He didn't want me to go. What should I do? I looked at the sunshine now streaming through the window, drying the last drops of melted snow.

'Don't run away again, Timba,' said Leroy, as if he'd read my mind. He stroked me thoughtfully. 'We've got to sort your fur out . . . make you all nice and glossy again.'

A lot of talking went on over lunch, and Vati slept, but I kept awake, listening for clues, and watching the white light from the Spirit Lion who had settled along the back of the sofa where Rick and Leroy sat with trays on their laps. The Spirit Lion was waiting for something to happen, and it did.

Leroy took a mobile phone out of his pocket and showed it to Rick. 'I got a smartphone now,' he said proudly. 'Would you like to see my art work?'

'OK. Yeah . . . show me,' said Rick, with not much enthusiasm.

'It's awesome,' said Angie.

Leroy was flicking the screen, his eyes sparkling with excitement. 'I only do lions,' he said, and began to show Rick his pictures. 'These are the White Lions of Timbavati in Africa.'

Rick came alive. He stared at the pictures in stunned silence. 'You didn't do these, did you?'

Leroy nodded.

'They are . . . mind-blowing. Brilliant!' said Rick, and looked intensely at Leroy. 'So why the White Lions?'

'They came to save the world,' Leroy said, and he began to talk fast and passionately. 'There's only a few of them left . . . three hundred in the wild, and some are in zoos. In Africa they believe the White Lions came from the stars . . . Angie's reading me the book.'

'Oh I know about them, Leroy,' said Rick. 'I've been there. . .to Timbavati, and seen the White Lions. I went on a volunteer conservation scheme, when I was training to be a vet.'

Leroy stared at him in awe. 'I'm gonna go there when I'm old enough . . . aren't I, Angie? I'm gonna help the White Lions change the world.'

'I don't know about changing the world,' said Rick. 'But it changed my life, going there. I didn't want to come home. But it's not easy to raise the money, Leroy, and you need to be a strong person . . .'

'I don't care.' Leroy looked fierce. 'I'm a good survivor, aren't I, Angie?'

'But these pictures are extraordinary. They'd love them at the Timbavati Centre.'

'When I've got enough,' said Leroy, 'Angie's gonna help me frame them, and I'm gonna have an exhibition and sell them for loadsa money. Then I can buy a plane ticket and go to Timbavati and work with the White Lions.'

'You're deadly serious, aren't you?' Rick said.

'Yeah . . . deadly serious.' Leroy stared at Rick, and the light of the Spirit Lion was all around him. 'I don't want to do nothing else . . . and I don't care what anyone else thinks. No one's gonna stop me.'

His words were electric, and even Graham and Angie were listening to him, spellbound. And Vati's eyes were dancing all over the place, watching the sparks and the light of the Spirit Lion.

'I believe you,' said Rick. 'You're an amazing young man. How old are you?'

'Twelve.'

'Wow. You are so talented,' said Rick, 'and determined. I really believe you'll do exactly that . . . and good luck! I shall come to your exhibition, and I'll be the first to buy one of those incredible lion pictures.'

Leroy beamed. 'Can I have your mobile number, and your email?' he asked. 'I'll add you to my contact list. BUT,' he added, wagging his finger at Rick, 'those pictures are gonna be EXPENSIVE.'

My dilemma was solved for me very neatly later that day when Angie picked Vati up for a cuddle. 'Poor little Vati, he's so thin,' she said tenderly, and Vati stared at her intently. 'He's not himself, Graham. What's wrong with him?'

Graham sighed and started tapping his fingers on the chair arm. 'I'm afraid Vati has never been the same since Lisa had him de-clawed.'

There was a furious silence, and Angie's face went crimson.

'WHAT?'

Vati nearly jumped out of her arms with fright. Immediately she lowered her voice, and calmed him. 'It's OK, darling,' she whispered tenderly. 'Let me see those darling paws.'

Vati started to tremble again, and wriggled out of her arms. He came and sat with me, pressing himself into my fur as close as he could get.

He really needs me, I thought, and looked at the afternoon sunshine gilding the window. If we were going to escape, it had to be very soon.

'That's appalling,' Angie said. 'How could she? How did you allow it, Graham?'

Graham faced her angry eyes calmly. 'Lisa just did it, without telling me. She was paranoid about him scratching Heidi.'

'Poor, poor little Vati. I can't bear it!' Angie ranted on and on.

Graham listened kindly, and even dared to put his arm

around her shoulders. She shook him off. 'Don't touch me,' she flared. 'I'm so angry. You could have stopped her, surely. She must have said something.' Angie seemed to be boiling over with rage she had bottled up for years. 'You and THAT BLOODY LISA,' she stormed. 'She ruined my life, now she's ruined Vati's life. How would she like to be de-clawed and have her precious fingernails pulled out?'

Leroy sat cross-legged on the hearth rug, his hands stroking both of us, his eyes watching Angie. 'I got the answer,' he said firmly and both heads turned to look at him. 'Vati's going to be OK if he stays with Timba. Can't we take Vati with us?'

There was an uneasy silence. Angie looked at Graham. 'Well?'

Graham drummed his fingers faster on the chair arm. 'I love that little cat,' he admitted, 'but Leroy's right. Timba and Vati need to be together . . . Vati's already more alive since Timba came . . . so, yes . . . I'll let him go.'

Problem solved!

Vati and I were to travel together, in the luxurious basket . . . we were going home to live with Leroy and Angie. Over the blue hills, across the shining river, and through the dark forest.

I only wished that Graham was coming too. There was a loneliness that hung around him now, a desolation of the soul. Like the rest of us, he needed Angie. He'd made a terrible mistake and his life was in its shadow.

Graham and I had been buddies. And he'd stuck up for me against Lisa and her broom. I decided to go and say thank you to him nicely. Humans don't like their men to cry, but as I lay on his chest, gazing and purring, I could feel that his huge body was tight with tears. I tried, but he held on to them.

I expected Vati to go under the sofa when Leroy brought the travelling basket in, but his face brightened and he went straight over and inspected it. Then he walked across elegantly with his tail up and said a beautiful, courteous goodbye to Graham.

'I'll miss you, little cat,' Graham murmured, 'and ... please forgive me.'

Vati touched noses with him, and ran back to the basket. We sat in there, together, facing outwards.

Two black cats against the world.

Chapter Eighteen

CHANGING THE WORLD

Vati and I are ten years old, Angie says, and we've just had our birthday. My fur is glossy and well brushed, and I'm still the best cat in the street. Vati has learned to play again, and we have mad half-hours in our happy home. On moonlit nights, the forest calls to me, but I won't go there. I'm a support cat, and my job is to care for Vati, Angie and Leroy.

Leroy is a young man now, and he's very rich, he tells me. He sold lots of his wonderful lion pictures and saved all his money. But early this morning he was packing a big rucksack, and he picked me up and said goodbye! And he said, 'Thank you! Thank you, Timba. You been my BEST, BEST friend.'

I sat in the window and watched a minibus pick him up at the door, and Angie was crying and crying.

Now it's nearly noon. The sun is high, and Angie is standing in the garden with Vati and me in her arms. I wonder why she's watching the sky so intently.

Suddenly she stiffens.

'That's it!' she says, and points to a shining plane that is climbing up and up into the blue sky.

Angie is still full of tears. I lick one from her cheek. 'Don't worry, Timba,' she says. 'These are happy tears. Tears of joy. I'm so happy for Leroy, and so proud of him. But we'll miss him, won't we, guys?'

We watch the shining plane until it becomes a bright bead, trailing a white arrow of smoke.

And finally, Angie tells us what is going on.

'That's Leroy's plane,' she says. 'It's taking him all the way through the blue sky to Africa ... to Timbavati to work with the White Lions.'

Angie was unusually quiet after Leroy had left. Her bright flame seemed to have gone out. She only came alive when we were looking at her laptop, Vati and I sitting on the table beside her, our heads weaving from side to side as we saw pictures of Leroy onscreen. Running down the steps from a big aeroplane and climbing into a truck with some other young people. 'He's making friends ... at last!'

Angie said. 'He's found kindred spirits.' But Leroy's eyes were homesick as he talked to Angie. 'I miss you, Angie, and Timba and Vati.'

When we finally saw the White Lions onscreen, we were awed. They looked so sumptuous and huge, powerful but relaxed. We cats were proud. Proud to belong to the global family of cats. The White Lions had come to change the world ... but so had we, and we had one more job to do ... for Angie.

'She's lonely,' I said as the two of us gazed into the embers of the fire. 'We've got to do something.' I thought about the journey I had made through the forests and across the shiny river. Was I too old to try again? And how would Vati cope?

He picked up my thoughts immediately. 'Don't even think about it, Timba.'

'I've got to fetch Graham,' I said. 'Whatever it takes.'

'No, Timba!'

But I got up and stretched, ate the rest of my supper, and headed out through the cat flap into the moonlit garden. Facing south, I searched the sky for the brilliance of that star on the lion's paw. My tail quivered. I saw the star. And that homesick longing filled my heart. I wanted my old home. I wanted Poppy, and the apple tree. But most of all I wanted Angie to be happy again.

I had to fetch Graham.

I remembered the maze of streets, the field of cattle, and the endless magical forest.

I set off down the road to the south.

Vati pelted after me and sprang in front of me like a dragon cat. His lemon-green furious eyes confronted me on the moonlit pavement. He wasn't going to let me go.

I sat down and felt my angry tail swishing to and fro over the tarmac. If my little brother thought he could stop me, I'd beat him up. My ears went flat, my fur bristled, and I hissed at Vati. To my astonishment he hissed right back at me, and the hiss lingered in the air between us. I tried to dodge around him, but suddenly Vati turned into a wild, hooky-looking demon. Even without his claws, he towered over me, the white moonlight glinted on his teeth, the orange street lights glazed the fur along his spine.

I hesitated. I wasn't scared of Vati. In a way I was proud of him. He hadn't got claws, but somehow he'd made himself strong enough to challenge me. He believed in his own power. And judging by the speed and sting of the swipe he gave me with a long whip of a paw, he was going to use it. On me!

Instead of fighting back, I sat there and looked at him until he calmed down. We studied each other's eyes. 'I won't let you go, Timba,' he said. 'There is a better way.' Still focused on my journey, I looked at him in silence, thinking I could sneak away later while he was asleep.

'There is a better way, Timba,' he repeated. 'Just because you are in a physical body you don't have to settle everything physically. Why go on that long journey when you can use your cat power?'

I stared at him. Cat power? All I'd done for the last few years was roll around on the hearth rug, purr and eat. People kept saying I was too fat.

'Follow me,' said my streamlined, velvet-coated, assertive brother, and he led me through the front garden and round the side of the house to where the old stone glittered in the starlight. We sat down, side by side, facing south. 'Talk to me,' I said, fearing Vati was going into one of his mysterious trances.

'Remember the golden roads?' he said. 'We're on one, right now . . . you used to sit here, Timba, when we were apart, and I heard every one of your messages, even though I didn't answer. I heard you. I saw you. And I felt you!'

The mist cleared from my mind, and I remembered the great white Spirit Lion who had come to help me at those times. The remembering was a nice feeling, like coming home. So I stayed close to Vati, our bodies trembling a little as we picked up the energy of the golden road.

'You do the purring,' said Vati, 'and I'll send the message. We're a good team. We'll send Graham a message.'

265

I don't know how many hours we sat there on the golden road in the moonlight, but suddenly I could feel sadness. A grey emptiness, a yearning, and it was coming from Graham. He wasn't singing. The lid of the piano was shut. Graham wasn't moving. He was slumped in his arm-chair, staring into space. The way Vati had been. Numb.

For three days nothing happened. Except that Vati was now the boss, not me. He'd kept me firmly inside, out of the rain that wrapped the house in veils of pearl and silver. Angie came and went, and cuddled us, and watched the laptop for news of Leroy. I ate and slept, and rolled on the rug.

It must have been a weekend, because on the third day Angie got ready to go to work. Her mood was ominously dark as she stacked the children's books and crammed them into a bag. I perched on the table and looked at her. I felt anxious. Something was going to happen. I could feel it through my fur. So strongly that I thought it justi-fied an amplified extended-meow.

'What's the matter, Timba?' she asked, and I did another one. I stood up on my back legs and put my paws on Angie's chest. I stared at her. Her breathing changed and she started to cry. 'You know, don't you, Timba?' she said, stroking me on both sides of my face. 'You're such an understanding cat. I really don't want to go to work today. But I HAVE TO.' She picked up her car keys and left.

I worried about Angie all morning until the sun came out, sending shafts of warm light through the windows. Vati and I looked at each other. We knew an overgrown garden where we could mess around and catch mice, even if I ended up catching them for both of us. We set off down an alleyway and under a broken gate, and spent the afternoon in the long grass, playing with the nodding seed heads and grasshoppers.

I wasn't relaxed. Part of me was listening, sensing change and it had heavy footsteps. Strange in a town where hundreds of people were walking around, but my sensitive mind focused on those particular footsteps.

'We should go home,' I said, and Vati led me back through the broken gate and down the alleyway. We both knew something at home had changed. It spooked us, and we ran, low to the ground, our whiskers twitching.

At the corner of the street, Vati turned and looked at me with frightened eyes. 'You stay here,' he said. 'I'll creep to the gate and check this out.' Alarmed, I watched him slink along the pavement to our front garden. I saw him peep round the gatepost and his neck stretched out with fright. He came charging back with his fur all stiff.

'What's wrong?' I asked.

'There's a man sitting on the doorstep,' hissed Vati.

'I sensed him all day,' I said, remembering the footsteps.

'What shall we do?' Suddenly Vati was like a scared kitten again, his winsome face waiting for me to lead him. I thought about the man on Angie's doorstep. It could only be ... my tail went up by itself. 'Come on,' I said, and Vati followed as I trotted confidently along the pavement. My tail waved in the air behind me like a plume of joy. I knew that my eyes were sparkling like suns, my heart buzzing with anticipation.

I paused by the gate to arrange myself for a grand entrance. With my fluffy coat flowing, I shone in the sun as I trotted faster and faster down the path, doing purr-meows at the man on the doorstep. I felt like the most powerful cat in the Universe.

And I was right.

It was Graham. On the step beside him was a bunch of red roses. 'No, Timba,' he said as I patted the crinkly cellophane. 'Don't shred the paper. These are for Angie ... my Angie,' he added, and then asked me a question. 'Do you think she'll have me back?'

I did a yes-meow.

I couldn't wait for Angie to come home. Vati and I sat on Graham, keeping him firmly under control in the afternoon sunshine. Until, at last, we heard Angie's quick bright footsteps on the pavement. I was anxious then. Would she fly into a rage and tell Graham to go away?

Angie had been angry with Graham for so long.

Graham got to his feet, the bunch of roses crackling in his hand. He looked suitably shamefaced, but it was only a mask. I knew in that moment that love was stronger than anger. I watched it change on Angie's face. When she saw Graham she paused in disbelief. Her school bag fell to the floor, its heavy burden of books spilling across the path. A smile dawned on her face and she ran to him, almost crushing the roses in a huge hug. Graham looked pleased, and I saw a tear sparkling in the corner of his eye.

'Angie . . .' he breathed.

Vati and I weaved and purred around their legs as Angie gazed up at Graham and into his eyes. 'Does this mean what I think it means?' she asked.

'Angie,' said Graham again. He searched for the right words. I did a purr-meow to encourage him. 'Will you have me back?' he asked nervously. 'I made a terrible mistake, letting you go like that. I've regretted it so much. Please . . . could we start over?'

If cats could cry, I'd have cried with happiness when the smile reached Angie's eyes and she gave a scream of joy. 'Thank you, Universe!'

'Does that mean yes?' Graham enquired.

'Yes. A million times yes!'

I knew then that we'd be going home.

Vati and I exchanged knowing looks. We'd cracked it! We didn't follow Angie and Graham into the house. We sat on the doorstep, proudly, guarding the love-nest. Two black cats against the world.

Acknowledgements

Thank you to my brilliant agent, Judith Murdoch, my patient editor, Jo Dickinson, and the team at Simon & Schuster UK. I would also like to thank Anne Pennington for building my website, my fantastic writers' group for their support, and my husband, Ted, for his kindness.